ASHES & DUST

Bloodlust Book One

by

J.M. Adele

Ashes and Dust

J.M. Adele © 2018

All rights reserved

Edited by Lauren Clarke
Cover Design by Book Flare Publishers
Cover photo from Deposit Photo © Olena Kucher
Separators from Vecteezy.com
Proofed by Fiona Dreaming Proof Reading and
Formatting
Formatted by Book Flare Publishers

Print Edition

ISBN: 978-0-9944516-4-4

This one's dedicated to my parents.
I know you squirm in your seats when you read my words, but you support me anyway and that means the world.
And I wish you wouldn't read them.
Seriously.
Stop.

Contents

Chapter

One

Alone

"Hey. Wake up." Leaning on her elbow, Shiloh reached over to jostle Seth's shoulder. She pushed her hair out of her eyes, squinting as the first rays of dawn crept through the crack in the curtains. Her boyfriend needed to get his sweet butt out of the window and down the drainpipe before her parents discovered their little secret. Sneaking around in the dead of night added a bit of thrill to the relationship, but she didn't want to get caught. Ever. She wouldn't be able to deal with the disappointment on her parents' faces as her dad spun her broken halo on his finger.

"Seth," she hissed, trying again. "You've gotta go. I'm leaving soon."

"Hunmpth." The pillow muffled his reply as his hand trailed over her flimsy camisole to land on her boob, giving it a squeeze. She didn't have much, but he didn't seem to mind.

Grinning, she stretched down to tap him on the ass before rolling out of his reach and out of bed.

"Where're you going?" Hugging the pillow, he lifted a sleepy eyelid and pumped his hips into the mattress a couple of times.

Insatiable. She almost licked her lips, not minding the idea of going another round at all, but she had to get to training. If she wanted a gold medal, she had to make sacrifices. She felt guilty enough about indulging in his company a few nights a week, but hell, she deserved it. And he *was* irresistible.

"You seriously need to go. If my dad catches you, he'll get his gun."

"Your dad loves me."

"My dad thinks we're both still innocent."

Seth snorted and reached up to scratch his head. "He's not that gullible, Shi. I'm pretty sure your sister knows what's going on, and there's no holding her tongue."

Lanie knew, but she was cool. They had a deal. She wasn't going to say anything as long as Shiloh drove her to whatever party she wanted. Lanie was set on getting the full high school experience. Lord knows why. Besides,

Shiloh had cleaned her sister's vomit one too many times. Lanie wouldn't dare say anything about Seth's visits.

"Well, if he's willing to pretend, then I am, too. I don't want to have *that* discussion with him."

Seth blinked a couple of times before his gaze trailed down her body, pausing at her chest and lingering at the juncture of her thighs.

She rested one hand on her hip. "If you don't leave now, I'm locking you out for a week."

His eyes shot up to hers as his mouth flattened out. "Okay. I'm gone." He hauled ass out of bed, into his clothes, and had one foot out the window before leaning in to peck her on the lips. "I was never here. Have a good swim."

Within a minute, he was across the street and out of sight, back in his own house.

She leaned on the sill, a pleased smile tugging on freshly kissed lips, and her heart thumping for the boy across the street.

———

Water slid like silk over her skin as her body glided through the pool. The burn in her muscles had long since faded—she'd reached the sweet spot. A point where her body was a machine in control, and her brain surrendered to wayward thoughts, the chemical blend of endorphins and adrenaline injecting that invincible feeling. She could do another hundred laps, easy, but she had an exam to study for. Only two more weeks until school finished, and

she'd be free to concentrate on her training over the summer before her senior year.

Her teammates had abandoned the pool an hour before, after their coach was a no-show. So what if they didn't do their normal training routine? She had the pool all to herself. Her hands cut through the cool crystal liquid with ease, the rhythmic lapping of each stroke and her timed breaths the only sounds she had to contend with. No shrill whistle. No yelled instructions. No splashing from the lanes beside her. Blissful solitude.

Shiloh smiled all the way through another five laps. She'd smoked their butts in the sectionals and was the only one to qualify for the Summer Nationals. She was faster, stronger, and more disciplined and determined than any of those flakes. She had her eye firmly set on World Championship selection. And in 2020, Olympic selection. She was going to Tokyo, baby.

Tumbling forward for the final turn, she kicked her legs and punched her arms out in long, sure strokes, pushing her speed to the limit before reaching for the wall. Lifting her head, she gasped for a breath, her eyes automatically seeking the timer on the wall. The triumph of beating her personal best was a heady drug rushing through her veins and hitching her cheeks.

Her satisfied smile was short-lived, her brow tightening as the eerie fingers of a strange presence danced along her skin. She strained to see through the beads of water running over her goggles, her labored breaths coming in short bursts of fear rather than from exertion. Light reflected off the rippling water, throwing moving shapes across the ceiling and walls. Shadows sought new

hiding spaces on the periphery of her vision. Shiloh tried to track each one. To map each shape. Define the source. But they were too fast, eluding her encumbered eyes.

For a split second she thought she saw the shadows merge into a dark figure lurking just beyond the blocks. Those eerie fingers gouged a little deeper, massaging her heart into a seizure. What the hell? A bolt of terror tore down her back and she threw her hands up to rip off her head gear, gripping it in a tight fist. Blinking as she scrubbed her face with her other hand, she searched the pool area.

Nothing.

I'm being stupid. There's nothing there.

She swallowed, unconvinced, because her gut was screaming, *'Run!'*

It wasn't the first time she'd felt stalked. Three nights before she'd woken alone with a jolt to find her curtains flapping as they were sucked out of the window by the hot breeze. She always kept her window shut at night. The only reason she'd open the window after dark was to let Seth in, and those visits were always prearranged.

Maybe she'd forgotten to lock her bedroom door and her mom had opened the window to let in some air? She'd hoped her mom had opened it. Now she feared it hadn't been an act of parental concern, but a warning shot.

Three girls had gone missing last week on their way home from a party in Granada Hills. The TV churned out a new horror story every day. Yet another reason for

Shiloh to stick to her strict routine. Her little bubble of safety.

She feared it was about to pop.

Somebody was watching her.

Shiloh knew it as sure as if they had a grip on her face, breathing down her neck.

She spun around, the water forming a whirlpool around her. Her heart thundered as she darted her eyes back and forth. Her movements were jerky, spraying water in all directions. For some stupid reason the theme to Jaws started playing in her head.

"Hello?" Her shaky question echoed off the cold tile and concrete surfaces making it sound like she'd cried out a hundred times, desperate for a response when there was only a lurking threat.

Her head dipped under the water for a second, fatigue wearing her down. She fought her way up, spitting out water.

I need to get out of the water.

Tossing her goggles and cap onto the concrete, she slapped her hands flat on the side of the pool before heaving her weight up. She didn't make it out. A vise-like grip around her ankle dragged her back into the pool. *Fuck! This is it. I'm going to end up like those girls.* The latest horror story to grace TV screens. Bubbles spewed from her mouth as she searched underwater, but there was nothing to see. Kicking off the bottom, she rocketed herself up, a scream breaking free as she breached the surface. Wracked with tremors, she grappled for the side

of the pool. Whipping her head about, she found nothing. Tears began streaming down her face as she sobbed, fearing the worst.

A voice came from beyond her sight. "Marco . . .?" The deep rumble of death, announcing the hunt.

Oh, Jesus. Shiloh's eyelids cranked wide enough to rival a canyon. She paddled her arms like she'd forgotten how to swim. The distance to safety seemed interminable. A viscous waterfall ran over her lips as her sobs intensified. She couldn't bring herself to reply, or even question who was there. Warmth spread between her thighs as her bladder let go of control.

Finally, she grasped the tiled edge. Again, she tried to get out of the pool, throwing her elbows along the side and kicking her knee up to haul her weight free. Gasping for breath, she rolled away from the edge before scrambling to her feet. The hairs on her body stood on end, her skin crawling.

A great gust of air rushed at her, tipping her off balance, and she stumbled back. Pain crashed her system as the stab of something sharp bit into her neck, and a breath-stealing grip seized her body. Her eyes rolled up, unable to see. Sound escaped her reach, her ears refusing to work.

Deprived of those senses, her others amplified. The smell and taste of copper and salt filled the back of her throat. She gargled. Blood choked her airway. She was going to drown. Not in the pool. In her own blood.

A raging wildfire spread from her neck, rushing along her veins, intent on possessing every part of her. Her

mind couldn't conjure up the will to fight as it struggled to connect any thought through the haze. Unable to move or suck in air, consumed by nothing but excruciating agony, Shiloh's body went limp as the last dregs of energy drained away.

The only thing she could do was surrender.

She vaguely registered the vise on her body loosening, and a tearing at her neck as the sharp object was removed. For what seemed like several minutes, she remained suspended in the dark, weightless vacuum of her mind before the sickening crack of her body hitting concrete signaled her end.

Her soul was severed from its tether to this world.

Chapter

Two

Memorial

Lanie Howard ran a finger down the framed photo of her older sister, collecting some dust before rubbing her fingers together, sending it to dwell on the carpet. "She's not coming back. Face it, Mom. If they find her, she's going to need a body bag."

She focused on the streak she'd left on the glass rather than the smiling face of her sister staring back at her. She hadn't been able to evict the image from her mind for four weeks—dark hair in a high ponytail, dark eyes crinkled at the corners. The perfect, Californian high school girl. The photo could've been Lanie. Except for the

fact that Lanie had braces and was a year younger. And Lanie's name didn't belong in the same sentence as the word *perfect*. Seeing her sister's likeness in the mirror made her want to shatter the glass.

Or put a paper bag over her head.

Plastic would be better.

Lanie's school photo had once sat beside Shiloh's photo. Now, it had been demoted. Moved out of sight and replaced by one of Shiloh's swimming trophies, surrounded by flowers. They must've taken it from the school where it had been on display.

From the corner of her eye, Lanie witnessed her mom choke on a reply, clutching at her chest like it had been splayed open with a sternal saw.

"Why don't you shut up, Lanie? It's only been a month." Disapproval sheared off Seth's tongue in frosty drifts, sending a chill up her back.

Shiloh's boyfriend was a regular fixture on the Howards' sofa under normal circumstances, but from the time Shiloh had vanished he'd barely moved, apparently waiting for her to walk in the door and end the nightmare. Or maybe he was unable to tear himself away from worshipping at the altar her parents had erected above the fireplace.

Shiloh was the star everybody loved.

Lanie was white noise.

Turning her back on the mantelpiece, Lanie locked on to Seth's bloodshot stare. "They found all her stuff still in her locker and enough blood to fill a keg. It doesn't take

a rocket scientist to understand she was badly hurt. You're all kidding yourselves if you think she'd survive that."

Seth's hand clenched into a fist, and she watched his perfect features morph through the spectrum from pain to hate. *Good.* If he hated her as much as she despised him, maybe they'd finally be even.

"What the hell are you doing here, anyway?" Tossing an arm at the front door, she delivered the final blow. "Your house is that way. Go home. You don't belong here."

Seth glared. "Shiloh hates you—"

"Lanie! Go to your room. Seth, I think it's time you went home. Emotions are high. People are saying things they don't mean. Let's all just calm down." Her dad quelled their argument, putting a comforting arm around his wife as she wailed uncontrollably.

"Gladly." Lanie stomped off up the stairs, shame firmly wrapping its filthy fingers around her ankles, dragging her down.

She *was* a bitch. She was angry.

Furious at her envy of Shiloh.

Angry at her sister for abandoning her.

Disappointed in her family for sitting on their asses and doing nothing.

Why were they all in denial? They should be out there hunting for Shiloh's killer, not sitting around boosting Kleenex's profits.

Slamming the bedroom door behind her, Lanie launched herself onto the bed, stuffing her face into the pillow as deep as she could get. Maybe if she deprived her senses she'd stop the realization from solidifying; her sister was never coming back.

Shiloh was the only one who cared. She was the caution to Lanie's impulse. The sane to Lanie's crazy. The earth to Lanie's fire. Her sister was as much a part of her as one of her limbs.

Or, she had been. Until Seth.

He'd climbed through Shiloh's bedroom window and apparently into her heart. Shiloh had started walking around with a dreamy look in her eye and Seth's name constantly on the tip of her tongue. Her open-door policy was abandoned in favor of privacy behind a solid barrier. Lanie had stopped knocking after interrupting their lip-lock sessions one too many times. The view of her sister's swollen lips and mussed hair as she peeked through the door had formed a hollow pit in the younger sister's stomach. She could've traveled the length of the hallway a thousand times and she wouldn't have bridged the distance between them.

It had hurt more than it should. Being replaced. Truth was, Lanie had been mourning the loss of her sister for over a year. She'd lost a limb, the phantom pain constantly reminding her of the amputation. It would never fade.

Hauling her head back, she tried to drag in a deep breath, jealousy and guilt suffocating her more effectively than the pillow ever could. She loved her sister. She'd

never wanted anything bad to happen to her. She always thought they could heal their rift if Seth got out of the way.

Shiloh's never coming home.

Ugh. Snap out of it.

She'd criticized her family for impotently sitting by and here she was—drama queen—making it all about her.

She drew in a long, stuttered breath as an alternative occurred. She could catch the bastards who did this. And if she died in the process, at least she'd done something instead of sitting around pissing tears.

Staring at the window, she remembered all the times she'd watched Seth shimmy down the drainpipe. Lanie was a gymnast. And she did track. There was no reason she couldn't do the same.

Grabbing a backpack, she threw in her wallet and phone before sneaking down the hallway to her mom and dad's room. She found the spare keys to the Mercedes and two hundred and twenty-three dollars to add to her stash of just over five hundred.

Bingo. She had wheels and she had cash.

Moving to Shiloh's room, she locked the door behind her. Not that they'd come looking for her in there; the room had been left untouched since the police had searched through it after her sister's disappearance. Sliding the window open, she poked her head out. The distance between the drain pipe and window ledge stretched on like she was looking into one of those crazy mirrors at the fair.

Jeez, Seth must have extendable arms.

Straddling the ledge, Lanie shimmied her bottom as close to the side of the window as she could, stretching an arm towards the pipe. Sweat coated her curled lip, her stomach dipping a little in fear as she slipped, her efforts falling short by more than a foot. *Damn.* She pulled back, shoving her hair out of her eyes, and moved to stand on the ledge. This wasn't going to beat her.

Anchoring one hand and foot to the window frame, she leaned out. Only just managing to touch the pipe with her toes, she grunted in disappointment and yanked her body back to safety, taking some skin off her elbow on the white stucco wall.

Crap. She hissed in a breath. How the hell had Seth managed to do it so easily? He was taller than her, but he wasn't a gymnast. But then, she'd never shimmied down a drainpipe.

All the hot air she'd pumped herself with wasn't enough to help her float to the ground. Bravado slowly began to leak out like the blood from her fresh wound. Swiping at the warm tears wetting her cheeks, she expelled all the breath from her lungs and forced her shoulders to relax.

She could march right past the perma-wake-in-waiting, but that'd start a new battle she wasn't up to dealing with.

No, you're not going out.

No, you can't take the car.

You must stay here and wait for absolutely frickin' nothing to happen.

Screw them. They didn't need to know what she was up to. And she wasn't going to let them get in her way.

The wheel of chance slowed to a stop, the flapper landing on plan B.

Dashing to the bed, she gathered the pillows and threw them out of the window until they formed a good landing pad. She pulled the sheets from the mattress and tied the two together, attaching one end to the leg of the bed. Tugging on her makeshift rope, she smiled as it held firm. Now this she knew how to do.

Within seconds she was on the ground, running for the Mercedes parked in the driveway. She didn't exactly have her license, but she'd done Driver's Ed. She knew enough to get where she was going. All she had to do was put it in neutral and let it roll downhill on to the road. Her parents wouldn't see or hear a thing, thanks to the handiwork of their gardener and his hedge fixation.

She slammed the brakes too hard at the bottom of the driveway, lurching forward before the seatbelt yanked her back. Shaking her head, she turned the key. Lanie glanced up at the Spanish mansion, just able to see the elaborate wrought-iron balustrade of the second-floor balcony from the road. The sheet rope hung limply from Shiloh's window, a white flag of surrender and a desperate call for help all in one. Lanie wanted to floor the accelerator, her tolerance level dipping into the negative, but she held back. They'd figure out what she'd done eventually. Maybe they'd wonder where she'd gone, but running away was a totally different deal to going missing.

She'd probably be back before they noticed.

She stewed on that thought all the way to the high school. It took three laps of the crowded Boulevard High parking lot before she gave up and pulled the car onto the grass verge. *What the hell are all these cars doing here?*

Stepping out of the air-conditioned Mercedes, the sun's bite had her skin instantly slick with sweat. She gave her shirt a couple of tugs to fan herself before securing her backpack. Lanie headed towards the nearest building and cupped her hands around her face, peeking in a window. The desks were all in neat rows. Black scrawl covered the whiteboard. But there were no students. It wasn't even lunchtime. *There must be some event happening.*

She shook her head. Who the hell cared? *Focus, Lanie.*

Her search had to begin at the end—where they'd found her sister's blood.

She brushed the dust from her hands and jogged towards the gymnasium that housed the basketball courts and aquatic center. As she weaved around the buildings and past the football field, the breeze carried the sound of singing coming from the gym.

She veered off, cracking open the door to the locker room, and positioned herself at the entrance to the courts so she could peer in without being seen. Bodies were crammed tightly together, filling the bleachers. On the center court, a table covered in red cloth held a large framed photograph of Shiloh—the same photo that was on the mantelpiece, only this one was blown up to three times its size—garnished with floral decorations.

They were having a frickin' memorial service?

And again, with the flowers.

Shiloh hated flowers.

Why the hell hadn't Lanie been told about this? Why didn't her parents know? Or maybe her parents did know, but they didn't want any part of it because they were still in denial. Oh, yeah. She'd bet her left butt cheek they knew.

Jesus, wake up and smell the blood.

The music faded, replaced by papers shuffling and weeping. Nobody spoke a word. They all sat looking like giant rainclouds hung over their heads, pissing on their parade. *Oh, please.* None of them really knew Shiloh. They all wanted to be her, and to be liked by her. But none of them ever got that close. Shiloh just made them think they did. They were in shock, that was all.

Madeline, one of Shiloh's teammates, stepped up to the microphone. Lanie's shoulders locked and her teeth ground together as she remembered Madeline shoving her head into a toilet on her first day as a freshman. *Bee-otch.* Lanie could almost smell the overdose of Wonderstruck from her hiding place.

Aside from the tragic spray tan, Madeline was Malibu Barbie with an extra layer of muscle. She'd been Shiloh's biggest competition since elementary school.

"Hello—"

The shrill squeal of feedback pierced the air as hundreds of hands flew to block ears. Madeline grabbed

the mic and moved away from the speakers while some guy fiddled with the amplifier.

"Let's try that again. Hello, everyone. Thank you all for coming to farewell one of Boulevard's best and brightest stars." She pushed her hair behind her shoulders and began to strut along the sidelines, obviously soaking in the fact that all eyes were on her. "I'm sure most of you know me. My name is Madeline Grant. Shiloh was my teammate, and my best friend."

Lanie had to cough at that, moving back farther into the shadows.

"When I heard the news, I was absolutely devastated. It's a shock I'll never recover from." A manicured finger reached up to dab away invisible tears. "I wanted to give all of us, those who adored her, a chance to say goodbye and celebrate her life in our own special way."

Lanie watched the Z-grade performance, almost convinced there were actual tears. Madeline's gal pals were doing just as awful a job in the stands, clutching at each other and churning through the Kleenexes. Listening to Madeline drivel was about as enjoyable as the acoustic feedback from earlier. Lanie plugged her fingers in her ears, expecting to find a trail of blood dribbling out.

Blood.

She had to get to the pool and check out the scene. The place would've been scrubbed clean by forensics, but maybe she'd find something. They didn't know Shiloh. Maybe she'd left some clue. She just needed to see it. See where her sister's life had ended.

Lanie took three steps towards the exit before an uproar sounded from the gym. Spinning around, she lurched for the door.

Her eyes squinted, unsure of the shift in reality.

What—

I can't—

She dropped her ass on the floor. Her jaw hung loose on its hinge as a tsunami of emotion carved a hole in her chest.

Impossible.

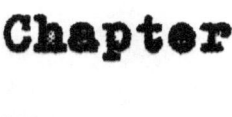

Chapter

Three

Amnesia

Covered in dirt and streaked with blood, Shiloh stumbled into the gym, still wearing her swimsuit. With her hands twisted together and her eyes as wide as dinner plates, she wondered what she was doing here. Her thoughts formed a twisted pile of metal. A car crash blocking the flow of consciousness. Her body followed a compulsion, denying her any control. There was something here she needed. Nothing her mind understood, but something her body implicitly sought to ease the hollow in her gut.

      She stirred up pandemonium with every lurching step, the crowd spilling from the stands. They came close,

openly staring, but nobody reached out. Whispers followed her . . . *She's a mess. What the fuck happened to her? Someone cover her up.* Their message bounced off the membrane of her eardrum but didn't sink through. The onslaught of noise and chaotic movement sucked the breath from her lungs and turned her legs to blocks of ice, but she pushed on. She was still locked firmly in survival mode.

Her eyes wildly searched the crowd for . . . who the hell knew? Familiar faces seemed to fly at her before something in her demeanor pushed them back.

The crowd slowly parted, opening a corridor as she stumbled towards the locker rooms. Her gaze locked on a pair of eyes so similar to her own. *Sister.* Her brain knew the connection, but the emotion that should've accompanied the recognition was lost in a void somewhere. The need to find *it* consumed her in a frenzy, and chased Shiloh's rational mind until it was a cowering fraction of the whole in one corner.

What Shiloh's body sought suddenly became clear.

She finally reached her destination. Planting her feet either side of her sister's knees, she looked down at Lanie's fragile form, folded awkwardly on the floor.

"Where is he?" The hard crust coating her vocal cords crumbled off, pulverizing her words to ash. The last time she'd made a sound it had been a glass-shattering scream. She hacked out a cough and tried again. "Where is he?"

Lanie blinked and ratcheted her body to stand. "Who? What happened to you? Where have you been? How are you even alive?"

"Shut up!" If she had any spit, it would've sprayed from her mouth. "Where is Seth?"

The gym doors slammed open as Seth barged in. "Shiloh!"

Whipping herself around, Shiloh was flooded with relief. *He's here. He'll take care of me.* Her parents scurried along behind him. She spared them a fleeting glance before toppling into his arms.

Shiloh's chest slowly expanded back to normal. The ice melted from her limbs, leaving them limp. She clung to him like he was a lifebuoy. The frantic drive to find what she needed began to fade as her body surrendered to exhaustion.

"You came back to me." Seth's broken whisper hit the side of her neck, and a shiver rolled down her spine.

"Always," she mouthed, unable to get her voice to work. Her arms came to life for a second, enough to give a squeeze before going limp again.

She had nothing left.

"Let's get out of here."

"She needs a hospital," her dad protested.

"No. Home." A force came through Shiloh's voice from somewhere unknown, dropping it an octave, and her dad reared back, his jaw loosening.

I'm not going to any goddamn hospital. Seth. I just need Seth.

Her boyfriend lifted her into his arms, carrying her out to her dad's car. Through heavy lids, she watched the distraught faces of her family as they scrambled after them. Her mother's hand smoothed the hair off her forehead, searing her skin like a hot brand. Shiloh hissed and jerked away, propelling her mom into a fit of despair, her face crumbling as she reached her arms out for an unrequited embrace. She couldn't bring herself to care.

Something had detached inside her.

But her connection to Seth had grown tenfold. A powerful energy drew them together. She didn't want anyone else touching her.

Ever.

Just Seth.

The trip home didn't register. She remained cradled in Seth's arms, the world around becoming a blur of shadows and light, echoes and pulsing.

Tucking her head into his neck, Seth lifted her out and took her into the house. The fragrance of lilies, roses, and magnolias assaulted her nose, and she pressed farther into his skin to quieten the nausea. They knew she hated flowers. Why would they do that to her?

Under her nose, she could feel Seth's pulse, could scent it through his skin, and flicked the tip of her tongue out to taste. Her eyes widened, her own pulse speeding up at the flavor. The deliciousness zinged across her taste buds and went down to stir the hollow at her center. She

couldn't help releasing a cry. It barreled out from the pit of her gut and whipped up a sandstorm in her dry throat. Shiloh's vision focused with the accuracy of a telephoto lens, able to see each pore, hair, and bead of sweat on that patch of skin at the side of his throat. She mapped the network of veins under the thin layer and saw the beat of his blood tick as it passed through the artery below.

"Shh, Shiloh. It's okay. Just a bit farther and you can lie down." Seth's baritone rumbled through the side of her face where she had it pressed to his cheek.

"What's wrong with her? Is she having a seizure?" Lanie's annoying screech clawed at her ears.

Seth pulled her quaking body closer. "She's probably in a bit of shock. I'll put her in bed. Do you have extra blankets?"

"Yes. Lanie, run and get them. Quickly."

Shiloh eyeballed her sister. With her hands pressed to her ears, Lanie's face was screwed up in pain. Beside her, their mother also blocked her ears, her face ashen as she stared back. Her father stood at the bottom of the stairs, looking up in horror.

They look like scared little mice.

I'm scared, too.

"Shiloh."

She turned back to Seth, zeroing in on the greens and browns flecked in his tawny eyes.

"You need to stop making that noise."

Cutting the sound off, she clenched her teeth together, but was shaking so badly they chattered.

Seth blew his dark blond hair out of his eyes as he whisked her into the bedroom and onto the bare mattress. Sheets hung out of her open window, tethered to the bed leg. Her mother scurried off to get pillows, and Lanie appeared in the doorway with blankets piled high in her arms. Seth swaddled her in the coverings and climbed on the bed beside her while Lanie looked on, chewing her fingernails. Her mom helped him arrange the pillows before reaching out to touch her forehead again.

Shiloh braced for the sting, snapping, "No!"

The woman wrenched her arm back, biting her lip as she gripped a hand around her throat.

Throat.

Whipping her eyes back to Seth's pulsing neck, Shiloh licked her lips, the shakes growing more violent. The periphery of her vision blurred as she focused on those two inches of his skin.

He swallowed. "Okay, guys. I think maybe we just give her some space."

Thump, thump, thump. The smooth skin jumped in time with the blood surging below.

Stretching a finger, she massaged the line of his artery, feeling it throb.

Throbbing. Surging.

Lanie butted in with her objections. "What about you? Why don't you back off so we can get near her?"

Seth's body tensed. "Lanie—"

Enough. Her vision tinted red. She shot her family a glare. "Get out!" Her whole body jerked. She was startled at the ferocity of her response.

What the hell was wrong with her?

Her family didn't stick around to find out.

That shrunken, cowering part of her consciousness clawed back to the surface, fueled by fear. Something wicked was consuming her, and if she didn't fight back she'd be lost forever. Searching Seth's eyes for the answer, she saw terror reflected back. She was scaring him, too.

"I'm sorry. I don't know what's happening to me." The words came out in pieces as her teeth chattered together.

"Shh. It's okay. It's going to be okay." He wedged his body between her and the headboard. Curling his arms under the blankets and over her shoulders, he smoothed his hands down to grip the back of hers before wrapping their entwined arms around her.

His lips touched the shell of her ear and he whispered, "Sleep, baby. We'll figure it out later. You're exhausted."

Yes, she was shattered.

She placed a kiss at his throat.

Suddenly the tremors stopped like all she'd had to do was flick a switch, and her eyelids dropped shut. The hollow in her belly filled with warmth and Seth rocked them side to side, humming until she slid . . . into . . . sleep.

What—

Lanie couldn't even put her thoughts in order enough to form a question.

That was—

She stood out in the hallway, staring at her sister's closed bedroom door. Her parents flanked her, gob smacked faces pointed at the solid wood. Everything on the other side of that door had gone quiet. Had Shiloh passed out? What the hell was going on?

The image of Shiloh in her torn, filthy swimsuit was tattooed on Lanie's corneas. God, she'd been wearing the same thing all this time. That was abuse enough in Lanie's mind, but what else had been done to her sister? It was a miracle she'd survived. But a person didn't just walk away from a terrifying experience unscathed. Lanie's heart cracked as she thought of the mental battles Shiloh would have to fight in her nightmares. Clearly, she wasn't herself. If Lanie had been abducted and managed to escape, the first people she'd run to would be her family. Despite all their issues, Lanie still loved them. She just wanted to be loved by them in return. Shiloh had stared Lanie down like she was nothing. Just a way to get to the one she wanted—*Seth.*

'Where is he?'

Lanie took the question like a sword through the heart.

When Shiloh walked into the gym, she'd barely been able to stand. Why hadn't she gone to the hospital, or the police station? Or home? That didn't make sense.

"I'm calling the police. Or an ambulance. Someone, anyone. This is ridiculous."

"We'll call in a doctor." Her mom shook her head. "Just let her rest. The police will want to take her away for questioning, and we only just got her back."

Lanie cranked her neck to squint at her mom, her hand twitching with the desire to slap her awake. "Are you serious? Didn't you see her?" She huffed, leading the way down the stairs.

"Lanie, I've had just about enou—"

Several car doors slammed before there was a knock at the door, cutting off her father's rebuke. Two dark figures crowded their porch, visible through the mottled glass entry.

"I bet it's the cops."

A splash of color moved beyond the figures, stirring a din. As her dad opened the door, ushering in the two detectives that had been assigned to Shiloh's case, Lanie's heart dropped in time with her mother's gasp. The street in front of their house was abuzz with activity. Several news vans from the major networks, parked nose to tail, their satellite dishes pointed to the heavens. Perched on at least ten shoulders, video cameras pointed at tailored individuals clutching microphones as their mouths moved. Cameras set off in an endless burst of prying clicks, and reporters shouted invasive questions as

they rushed at the door before it was slammed in their faces.

"Mr. and Mrs. Howard, it has been a little while. Sorry for the intrusion. We'll get a couple of officers to man your front yard and keep the media at a reasonable distance. We had hoped to deliver some good news the next time we saw you, but I hear you're the ones able to deliver on that hope. Is she here?"

The pair of detectives posed an odd combo. The shaggy-haired, blond surfer dude, and his sleek brunette, female partner. *Dumb and Dumber,* revamped for a generation bent on equality.

"Yes, she is, but she's resting. Have a seat. Can I get you anything?"

Lanie's mouth pinched tight. Her mother—the consummate hostess. These idiots hadn't done a thing to help find Shiloh. They'd come to a dead end and given up. Useless. They didn't deserve the hospitality.

Lanie let her eyes roll and followed the group into the living room.

"No, we're fine, thanks." Surfer dude, pulled at his tie.

They unbuttoned their jackets and sat in perfect synchronization. It was almost comical except for the fact that they should've had the door shoved in their faces, like the media scum.

The blond guy spoke again. "We have several witnesses who caught Shiloh's return on video. I'm afraid it's already on social media. We can't do anything about

that, but we are concerned for her health. If possible, we'd like to gather some forensics. She'll be examined by medical personnel trained in medico-legal exams."

"What does that mean?" Her mother's jaw wobbled, eyes popping.

"She's obviously suffered some physical trauma. We can't rule out abuse of a sexual nature. We'll need to question her as soon as possible. We may gain valuable insight into what happened to her, and the identity of the perpetrator who committed these crimes against her, by collecting evidence from her person."

Lanie pulled up an image of Shiloh and morphed it into a walking petri dish. Nameless, faceless, and ready to incubate at their convenience. "So you're going to strip her and poke and prod around looking for evidence when she's already suffered God knows what indignities? There's a video of her stumbling around looking like she's been dragged backwards through the woods. She's almost naked, for Christ's sake."

Her father's hand landed on her shoulder in silent warning.

"This is our job. I know it's unpleasant, but if we're going to find out who took her, and what happened, we need to start with Shiloh," the brunette said.

"I'll take you to see her."

"Thank you, Mrs. Howard."

Jostled awake by the hard cushion of Seth's body moving from underneath her, Shiloh groaned and rolled to her stomach as he went to answer the soft knock at the door.

"Seth, the detectives are here to question Shiloh." She could barely hear her mother's whisper.

"But she only just got to sleep."

"I'm afraid they're insisting."

Shiloh squinted behind the strands of hair shielding her eyes, searching through the fog inside her head for an explanation as to why the LAPD were here.

"Shi?"

Expelling a grunt, she twisted her head to the other side, pain slicing through her neck. "Aargh." In an effort to get comfortable she pushed up to her elbows, gasping as her whole body awoke in an uprising of aches.

"Hey, take it easy." Seth's voice reached across the room.

Kicking off the blanket, she turned onto her back. Shiloh saw her mother frozen in the doorway, clutching at her neck. "Give us a minute, Mom." Hearing him shut the door, she turned watery eyes on Seth. "God, it hurts. Why am I sore all over?"

Lifting her hands, she noted the dirt caked under her fingernails and ground into her skin, as if she'd had a bath in the stuff. Wrenching upright, she whimpered as she saw her bloodstained swimsuit and torn up feet. Fear and confusion spiked her pulse. The evidence of a harrowing experience was plastered in splotches all over her body,

but she had no memory to connect the dots. "What the hell happened to me?"

"Baby, that's what we'd all like to know. The police are here to talk to you. Are you okay to do that?" Stroking her cheek with the back of his fingers, Seth lowered to his knees and kissed her forehead. "I can ask them to give you more time."

His touch diffused the rising panic, bliss flowing to her every cell. Dropping her palms to her knees, she swayed towards him, enjoying the rush. The fog in her memory cleared away as the sight of him flashed her thoughts back to the moment she'd noticed him moving in across the street. Riding home from an early training session, she'd eyed the removalist's van, curious who would want to live in a house that had seen more break-ups and death than any house should. The place was cursed for sure. And then this golden god had stepped out onto the lawn and looked right at her. She'd wobbled for about ten yards before jumping off and running her bike up the driveway. That entire Saturday had been uncharacteristically wasted staring out her window, committing every glimpse of him to memory. The way his muscles rippled as he shifted each box. How he'd swiped at his golden hair every time it fell across his forehead. The fact that he'd gone for a joyride up and down the street when he'd offloaded his bicycle instead of storing it immediately. And every time his eyes had strayed in the direction of her house. Maybe he'd been curious about her, too.

"Shi?"

"Huh?"

"Are you able to speak to the police now, or should they come back later?"

Blinking, she paused to let the question register, each word eventually lodging itself in place.

"Now's fine," the response drifted off her tongue, unsolicited.

"Here, cover up. You can shower as soon as they're gone."

He backed away, and her state of bliss started to fade. She found a T-shirt and shorts in her lap and blindly put them on, her limbs stiff from—what? Disuse? Overuse? Abuse? She wiped away a tear, wishing she knew.

Seth opened the door for the pair of detectives. They stepped in, looking like the male/female version of *The Odd Couple*.

The woman's sharp green gaze locked onto Shiloh, uncaging the panic that Seth had only just managed to subdue. "Sorry to intrude. I'm Detective Carter, and this is Detective Simpson. We were hoping we could ask you some questions."

Shiloh dipped her chin before her eyes darted sideways to watch Seth heading for the door. Her hand snapped out to latch onto the back of his shirt so fast she didn't even feel it move.

"It's okay, baby. I'll just wait outside."

"No."

She pulled him back, the mattress bouncing as he landed beside her.

Er . . . she didn't think she'd yanked that hard.

"Do you want me to stay?" her mom squeaked from her post at the door.

Shiloh didn't spare her a glance. "No."

Detective Carter cleared her throat and shut the door before helping herself to the desk chair, while her partner stood, blocking the exit.

"Shiloh, we know you've been through an awful experience, but we need to ask you some questions, okay?"

"Mm." *No.*

"What do you remember about the day you disappeared?"

She sucked in a breath and grabbed Seth's hand as she ordered the memory to the surface. "I remember swimming."

This was okay; she could do this. The thrum of calm from Seth's touch did its thing while shadows lengthened over her recollections, darkness setting in for the rest. "I thought I was alone, but then I wasn't. Something grabbed me." She released Seth, her trembling hand flying to the side of her neck as her body relived the nightmare. "It stabbed me with something. I screamed. I remember screaming, and then . . . I blacked out." She swayed as her head clouded and seemed to disconnect from her body, her thundering heartbeat coming from a lower altitude.

The squeeze of Seth's hand brought her crashing back. Her spine went ramrod straight.

"Hey, hey, it's okay. You're okay, you're safe." He smoothed his other hand down her spine.

"I'll give you a minute." The detective examined her like she was locking away some truth for future reference.

"Yeah, thanks." *Whoa.* Whatever that sensation of separation was, she knew she'd felt it before, but worse. What had happened to her?

She shook her head and gave a wobbly smile to the detective, letting her know it was okay to continue.

"Do you remember any smells or sounds from your assailant?"

"I could only smell and taste blood. I cho—ked on it." Shiloh's shoulders rose with a drag of air.

"Did they speak to you?"

"Marco. It said Marco."

"*It?* Was the voice high-pitched, or deep? Male or female?"

"It. I don't know, I don't remember. The sound echoed. I panicked."

Detective Carter scribbled something on her notepad. "Okay. What about when you woke up? Do you remember anything about where you were?"

"Just now? I remember Seth talking to Mom."

Carter blinked with her pen poised on the paper. "No. Before you came back to the school."

Huh? "Did I go back to school?"

"Yes. You walked into your own memorial service. You don't remember that?"

"Memorial serv—" Shiloh pursed her lips, unable to finish the word as the need to cry stung the back of her throat. They'd all thought she was dead. She wasn't the only one who'd suffered torment. What a horrible experience this had been for her family. For Seth. She gripped his hand tighter, never wanting to cause him that worry again.

Detective Carter's brow bunched tight. "You have no recollection between passing out beside the pool and waking up here, just now?"

Shiloh shook her head, blinking back tears.

The detective leaned back on the chair, sighing. "Well, Shiloh, I have to be honest. We're concerned for your health. I think it will be best if you come with us so we can get you checked over. The trained staff can collect any forensic evidence during their examination."

"What does that mean?"

"We'll take some photos of your injuries, and some scrapings from under your fingernails. They'll look at you head to toe and take samples if needed. And we're going to need the clothes you're wearing and the blankets you just slept on, too. If that's okay? You can say no to any part of the examination at any stage, and you can have a support person present. Your mom, maybe?"

"No."

"But—"

"I'm not having a medical examination. I'll give you the clothes, but that's it. I don't want anyone touching me."

"I can't force you. But if something has happened to you that has permanent consequences, or even temporary damage, we need to get that seen to."

"I don't want anyone else touching me. Only Seth."

"Okay." Detective Carter reached inside her jacket and removed a large plastic bag. "Please put the clothes in this. I'll wait out here until you're done." Nodding to Seth, she cocked a brow. "Simpson has some questions for you, too. Maybe you could take it elsewhere?"

"Already on my way." Seth got to his feet.

She almost leapt from the bed to drag him back again. The thought of being separated from him sent a frenzy of fear spiraling through her system. Sweat coated her skin, her temperature soaring as air rushed in and out of her chest.

Seth. Come back, Seth.

Shiloh walked through the closet, closing herself in the bathroom, and averted her eyes from the mirror as she removed her clothing. She was stripped bare in a violation of everything she'd held dear. Someone or something had touched her and destroyed her. Their hands had been on her clothes, on her skin. Goose bumps rose over her body in a chilly tide.

She placed the flimsy material in a plastic bag. The electric blue straps of her bathing suit stood out with the

vibrancy she'd once had, somehow escaping the filth the rest of the suit had succumbed to. Looking at them, she had to suck in a breath.

She'd just discarded her old life into an evidence bag. There was no way she could get back in the pool. All hope for the Olympics gone.

Clamping it to her chest, she clenched her eyes shut so they couldn't leak. She still had Seth and her family. And if that small part of her old life had endured the filth and survived, maybe she could, too.

Putting on her bathrobe, she took the bag out to the detective. As she passed it over, their fingers touched. Shiloh froze, locking eyes on the wall, denying herself oxygen. *Seth, please come back. I need you.*

Detective Carter's concerned face filled her vision, her mouth moving, but no sound made it past the high-pitched ring in her ears. In a flurry of movement Seth was by her side, dosing her up with his antidote. She didn't know if Carter had everything she needed, but she didn't care. She just wanted to forget all this and move on.

Pulling a card out of her wallet, the detective passed it to Seth. "I'm going to leave my card with your friend. If you remember anything, anything at all, no matter how small, just let us know." She exited the room.

"Are you okay?" Seth squeezed her hand.

Nope. She wanted to scrub herself so clean until there was nothing left but bones. "I'm going to have a shower."

She hobbled to the dresser to pick out something new to wear.

"I'll wait here."

Her shoulders darted up. "Um—" She screwed her clean clothes into a ball and clutched them to her chest, shuffling her weight from one foot to the other. The urge to reach out and touch him, to get her hit, pulsed through her veins. "This is probably a weird request, but I don't think I can do this without you. I mean, not in the shower with me, but I'd feel better if you were in the room."

His lips quirked on one side, but his eyes showed an intensity that made them swirl with colors. She couldn't look away from their mesmerizing dance.

"It's not weird. I'd feel better if you never left my sight again, so we're even." Sliding an arm around her shoulders, he led her to the bathroom, standing behind her as she studied their reflections.

She was filthy. Underneath all the dirt she was certain there'd be bruises. Her neck ached the worst; she'd barely been able to move it, but with Seth rubbing the tender skin it seemed to be loosening up. Tilting her head to the side, she drank in his reflection, so transfixed she forgot why they were there. His skin and eyes shimmered under the LEDs, surrounding him in a halo of light. Or maybe it was her eyes playing tricks on her, or the drugging touch he plied her with. Every stroke of his skin on hers thrummed with an intoxicating energy. She wanted to melt into him, bend to his will. Give him whatever he wanted. Be whomever he wanted. He could guide her anywhere and she'd go.

Shiloh blinked as she got caught in the way he watched her. A hungry possessiveness competed with the adoration in his eyes and his embrace. She knew she was everything to him in that moment. But as she stared at her hollowed eyes and diminished reflection, she wondered what she had left to offer. She appeared as a ghost of her former self, while he had become resplendent and completely . . . addictive.

Reaching up to thread her fingers through his, she latched on, knowing she needed him more than he could possibly know.

More than even she could comprehend.

Chapter

Four

Darkness Himself

"Come on, Shi. It's been more than a month since you came back. It's time you got out of the house."

Lanie watched her sister rock gently on the edge of the bed as she stared at Seth's house across the street through the newly installed bars. Occasionally, Shiloh's hands would scrub up and down her thighs, or clutch her stomach before returning their grip to the mattress.

She barely ate. Almost never came out of her room. The mention of returning to the pool gained no

response. Shiloh might have come back in body, but her spirit was still trapped in some unknown hell.

The creepiest thing? Shiloh's eyes. They were lighter. Still brown, but a distilled shade, as if the absence of her spirit had drained them of color. It gave Lanie the chills.

Her sister still refused to see a doctor. She wasn't speaking to the psych their parents had insisted on. The cops hadn't found anything to explain what had happened to her. Not that they were telling the family, anyway. The only time Shiloh came alive was when Seth came to visit. It was like she needed him to push the buttons on her remote control to work. Their parents had decided to limit her time with Seth. When they told her, Shi went ape shit. Seth had managed to restrain her, taking her up to her room where she'd crashed for eighteen hours of sleep. If anything else gave Lanie chills, it was the pair of them, together.

She ran her tongue over her braces and cracked her neck. "You are coming with me to the mall. I need new shoes before school goes back, and I need your opinion."

Lame. Christ, Lanie, can't you do better than that?

Shiloh's hollow gaze slid to Lanie's feet for a second before lodging back on the window. Lanie took that as a good sign. Any reaction was better than this dormant zombie act her sister had going on.

An idea came to Lanie as she wracked her brain for the hammer that would break through the glass cage Shiloh was trapped in. "Seth said he'd meet us there, but

you have only ten minutes to get ready because you've been sitting on your a—"

Aaand, there we go.

It was cruel to lure her sister by dangling a treat Lanie wasn't going to deliver, but she wasn't above using dirty tactics.

Springing to action, Shiloh pulled her hair back in a ponytail and threw on a strapless summer dress. Wow. Zombie to babe in sixty seconds.

Shouldering her way past, Shiloh didn't waste any more time. "Let's go."

———

The mall was packed with frazzled parents entertaining their bored children while soaking up some free air-conditioning. Groups of teens occupied seating areas, spewing commentary. Hardcore shopaholics hopped from boutique to boutique, getting their dose of retail therapy. And Lanie sat with her sister in a coffee house, wishing she'd let sleeping zombies lie.

"Are you sure you don't even want anything to drink?"

"You said he'd be here. Where is he?"

Lanie wanted to growl and smash her fist on the table, but she rolled her tongue along the metal of her braces and sighed instead. Shi had been through hell. Lanie needed to remember that. Nobody knew how they'd cope under traumatic circumstances until they were in the thick of it.

But sure as shit, I wouldn't be pining for a stupid boy.

"You know, ever since you've come back you're obsessed with your boyfriend. You used to have other things in your life. You had swimming, and family, and friends. Now you can barely stand up without him holding your hand. What the hell, Shi? Why do you want to see him so badly?"

"I—" Shiloh stopped, her attention grabbed by a commotion coming from the electronic store across the corridor.

"I'm calling security!"

Lanie could just see a balding, red-faced man through a gap in the huddle of onlookers. He looked like he was about to burst a blood vessel, madly flapping his hand as a smoke ring billowed around his face.

"Put out that cigarette. There's no smoking in here," the middle-aged man said.

"I didn't steal nothin'." Lanie couldn't see the man who'd replied.

Shiloh shot to her feet, nearly toppling her chair as she craned her neck to get a better view. Lanie watched her sister's face instead of the spectacle. The way she'd zeroed in on whoever was making trouble, her body angling towards him, Lanie half expected Seth to come swaggering over to their table.

But Seth wouldn't be caught stealing or smoking. The only daring thing he did was sneak in her sister's window.

A collage of emotions stirred Shiloh's features until finally she settled on confusion.

A shadow stretched over the table and climbed Shiloh's body. "What are you lookin' at? Show's over."

That was definitely not Seth's voice.

That voice held the promise of danger and sin.

Lanie tilted her head to take in their visitor, the cigarette still pinched between his thumb and finger. *Dark* was the word that came to mind. He had midnight black hair, tied in a low ponytail. Thick brows anchored low over eyes so dark the pupils were swallowed whole. Smooth brown skin stretched over the angles of his face, his chin partially hidden by a goatee. The guy wore jeans and a black long-sleeved Henley with a checked flannel shirt over the top. In summer. Like he was giving heat the finger. Anger radiated in a magnetic field around him as his eyes pierced into her sister. And Shiloh just stood there staring dumbly.

Lanie had the urge to jump between them, but the guy's head whipped around to check over his shoulder, breaking his grip on Shiloh. He sneered before turning back and dropping his cigarette on the carpet, stubbing it out with his boot. Shooting one last glance at Shiloh, he strolled away, disappearing into the crowd.

One of the baristas came scurrying over to scoop up the cigarette butt and clean the carpet. Shiloh tottered on the heels of her feet before landing stiffly on her chair, a crease between her brows.

Lanie shook off the encounter with Darkness Himself, chalking it up to shopper rage. The guy was

unhinged—the way he'd stared Shiloh down with super-heated intensity. He was like a star before going supernova. A gun without the safety on. Something to stay the hell away from.

"That was weird. Are you okay?"

"Hm." A flush fanned out across her sister's neck.

Seth seemed to materialize out of nowhere. Lanie's hand slapped on her chest, her heart jerking in fright. "Shit, Seth. Where did you come from?"

He slipped his hands onto Shiloh's shoulders as he leaned down to kiss her on the cheek. "Hey, baby."

Here he was again, hijacking her time with Shiloh. Lanie's eyes automatically traveled over his body before she pulled them back, grinding her teeth. Stupid asshole had some sort of animal magnetism, and she hated him all the more because she wasn't entirely immune.

"Morning, Lanie. I'm good. Thanks for asking." Seth curled one corner of his lip, pulled out a chair, and flipped it around to sit on it backwards. Turning away from Lanie, Seth addressed her sister, "It's good to see you out. Are you still waiting for your coffee?"

Stiff shouldered, Shi's hand locked on to Seth's forearm before her lips finally curved up, her shoulders dropping. "Hi."

Ugh. Excuse me while I gag.

"Hi." He returned her goofy smile before his face hardened. "Who was that guy?"

Shi's hand slipped off his arm, her chin dipping as her mouth clamped shut.

Lanie's brow creased before she jumped in to answer. "He was just some random loser." *Okay, she's acting super weird.* Maybe Shi had seen the stranger before. Why else would he have come to their table instead of taking off before security could catch him?

Flexing his fingers, Seth searched the shoppers as they wandered past the door. "He won't come back. Nobody looks at my girl like that and lives." He grinned and laid a kiss on Shiloh's lips. "I'm starving. What's on the menu?"

"Shiloh's not eating." Lanie didn't mean to snap, but who the hell invited him? Although, it was good to see Shiloh smile, even if it was through her green-tinged viewpoint.

"What? Are you sick?" Seth feathered his fingertips along her cheek and Shiloh practically purred at the touch. Lanie's stomach lurched as she watched on and coughed to cover it up. "Do we need to get you to the doctor?"

"No. I'm fine. I think I'd like a steak."

Lanie cocked a brow. "Steak? At ten in the morning? Yeah, well, they don't do that here."

"I'll cook you a steak if you come back to my place."

"Hold up. Mom and Dad won't let her go to your place."

"Then we'll eat at yours."

"Suit yourself." Lanie sculled the rest of her cappuccino before gathering her bag.

Seth stood, tucking her sister under his arm. "I'll take Shiloh home. We'll meet you there."

"I don't have my license yet, genius. Shiloh drove over here."

"Hasn't stopped you before."

"You're such a jerk."

"And you're a spoilt brat."

His words cut deep, bringing tears to her eyes. Why did she even care about his opinion?

Turning her cheek, she told her sister she'd wait at the car before weaving through the crowds to the elevator. Lanie punched the close-doors button before anyone could join her, setting free a deluge of pain as the lift ascended to the rooftop. She'd been keeping it all bottled up—the rejection, the loneliness, the despair, and the inadequacy. It had to come out sometime, right? *Spoilt brat*. Yeah, if being ignored meant you were spoilt, then she was that.

She put on her sunglasses, keeping her head down as she exited past the shoppers waiting to get in the elevator. Cars prowled the lot, vultures waiting to pounce on the next available space. The bright California sun hit her in the face as it bounced off multiple windshields, heating her already foul mood to a boil. Reaching the car, she slapped her hands on the roof, spun her back to the door, and slid down to squat. Releasing a spray of curse words, she smacked the back of her head against the metal, hoping she left a dent in its perfectly shiny exterior. It would be a visual cue for anyone still under the illusion that they were the perfect family.

"He ain't worth it."

Jerking sideways, she fell on her ass, letting out a squeal. The dark-haired guy stood over her, legs apart, taking a drag of a cigarette. What the hell? Had he followed her? She was all too aware that she was hidden between the cars. Nobody would see her unless they were driving past and looked to the side. All they would see was him having a smoke. The guy loomed large above her, radiating anger. His sharp features drawn tight, midnight eyes drilling into her, encroaching on her personal space. Her tears ran in rivers, frustration forgotten as danger took its place. His chest puffed out as he held in a lungful of smoke. Crouching down to her level, he made an *O* with his mouth and blew a sequence of smoke rings in her face.

Grimacing from the toxic onslaught, she held her breath, too scared to move. Why had he followed her? How had he followed her? She'd been alone in the lift. Unless he took the stairs.

"Stop crying. I ain't gonna hurt ya."

She doubted that with every bone of her body, their forms turning brittle. "Back off."

Smoke came out of his nose as he snorted. "Or what?"

"I've got a gun." She pushed the threat through a narrowed throat.

His features smoothed in a laconic mask. Casually, he raised his cigarette closer to his face, rolling it between his thumb and finger. He flicked the ash and took another drag before settling his black eyes on hers. "No, you don't.

Your dad's got a gun in a safe in your basement. But you . . . you're not old enough."

The bottom dropped out of her world. How would he know that unless he'd been watching them? Even then. He'd have to have been inside their house to know about the gun safe. She thought of Shiloh. Did this guy have something to do with her disappearance? Had he done something to her and now he was after Lanie?

Somebody help me!

The hot pavement bit at her hands as she scuttled towards the front of the car like a crab. "How do you know that?"

"I know a lot of stuff about you, Lanie Elizabeth Howard."

Chapter

Five

On the Hunt

"You fucking creep. Stay away from me. I'm calling the cops." She was barely able to speak. Her heartbeat hammered between her ears as she pictured her face illustrating the headlines. *'Pool of Blood Left Behind as Sister of Missing Girl Disappears.'*

"Oh, yeah? What are ya gonna tell them? That I threatened you with secondhand smoke?"

Please. Don't . . . "What do you want?" she sobbed.

"Nothin'. I don't want nothin' from you, or your sister."

"Leave her alone!"

Lanie's head whipped to the right. *Seth*.

He charged at the guy, fist first, landing a punch that knocked him over. Lanie sprang up and dashed around the other side of the hood where Shiloh watched on in shock.

The stranger unfurled to his full height, a couple of inches taller than Seth's six-foot two. Lifting his hand, he inspected his now broken cigarette, its tip hanging by the thinnest slice of paper.

Releasing another snort, he turned his gaze on the sisters. "He broke my smoke."

Is he joking right now?

As if in slow motion, Seth's fist went flying at the stranger's face again. It never hit its target, the guy snapping out his palm to catch it in his grip. Seth's body twisted in pain as he let out a grunt, and dropped to his knees, out of view. Lanie might've laughed at Seth's misfortune, but the fact was he'd come to her rescue. He was the last person she'd expected to stick up for her. Thank Christ he had.

The girls moved around in time to see the stranger bend to whisper something in Seth's ear. Seth jerked his head away before the guy turned to leave, calling over his shoulder, "Nice talking to ya, Lanie. See you at school."

School? What?

Shit. They'd be seeing him again. Who the hell was he?

'Nothin'. I don't want nothin' from you, or your sister.'

That was the biggest lie she'd ever heard.

Seth cradled his sore hand against his chest and got to his feet, his face red with anger.

Shiloh raced to her boyfriend's side. "What did he say?"

"He bit me."

What the frick?

Lanie heard Shiloh suck in a breath. "You're bleeding." Reaching up to his ear, she drew a bloodied finger back, swaying as she fixed her gaze on the blood running towards her palm.

Lanie's stomach almost folded inside out as she witnessed her sister poke out her tongue and lick her finger clean. Red spots flecked Shiloh's irises before the black of her pupils completely engulfed the whites of her eyes. She released the same feral cry she'd made after coming home.

Holy shit. Lanie's skin prickled all over, her jaw hanging loose.

"Shiloh?" Seth mouthed, holding his hands over his ears.

Shiloh's head twisted in his direction, the sinister black orbs showing no evidence of humanity. Her scream ceased, replaced by the distant sound of car horns blaring, crunching metal, and shattering glass.

Like she was attached to a bungee cord, Shiloh leapt backwards, landing on all fours on the roof of a car three rows back.

Jesus Christ. What the frick is happening?

"Shi!" Lanie started after her, though every muscle was coiled, ready to run in the opposite direction. A beast had emerged, but her sister was still in there somewhere. And Lanie needed to save her.

"Stay there. Don't come near me."

Even her sister's voice was unrecognizable, plunging to a gravelly depth. Lanie kept coming, and Shiloh took off. As fast as a bullet, she ghosted into thin air.

Lanie skidded to a halt in the middle of the lane, turning in circles to search the sea of cars. Heart pounding, thoughts scattering, the only clear thing she could think was *what the hell?*

What happened to you?

———

Seth drove Lanie back to his home in silence. In her head, she tried to write the script for the scene ahead. Her explanation of Shiloh's whereabouts to her parents. How could she tell them that she'd disappeared again? And why?

She kept her eyes glued to the windows for any sign of her sister while she chewed her fingernails until they bled. Truth was, she wasn't so sure she wanted to see

Shi at all. *Those black eyes.* They'd belonged to a wild animal. Lanie shuddered as she bit down too hard.

"Stop biting your nails."

"What do you care?"

"You're bleeding." Seth turned away, glancing out his side window. "If she's waiting at my place and sees more blood, what do you think is going to happen?"

Oh, shit. "Yeah."

What if she attacked his father? "Is your dad home?"

"No, he's away."

Seth parked around the back and turned off the car, not getting out of his seat. With his eyes closed, he spoke through gritted teeth. "You can wash up in the downstairs bathroom. There are Band-Aids in the cabinet."

Exiting the car, he slammed the door behind him, and jogged up the back steps.

Jeez, he was acting like it was her fault that Shiloh had gone feral.

What if her sister was watching her right now? *And I'm out here on my own.*

Fumbling for the door handle, she bolted up the steps, making sure to lock the back door behind her. Her fingers were a mess, blood smearing on the handle. She'd have to come back and clean that up after she found the bathroom. A bathroom. The house was so huge, she guessed it had several on each level, just like her place.

"Seth?"

No response. Unless he didn't hear her. He must've gone upstairs. He had his own first-aid to attend to.

Padding through the kitchen and living area, she headed for the hallway. Testing the doors, she located the laundry and a cupboard before she finally found what she was looking for. Lanie cleaned off the blood, using a Kleenex to dry her fingers and stop the bleeding before she caught sight of herself in the mirror. The lights drained her face of color. Or maybe it was the fact that her sister was some kind of monster. A monster who would be sleeping down the hallway from her, if Shiloh ever came home.

Oh my God. What if her sister was irretrievable, replaced by that blood thirsty thing? What if she came for Lanie in the night? What if Shiloh slaughtered the whole family and then skipped over the road to finish Seth off, too?

How did this happen? Was it an infection, or had her DNA mutated in some way? There had to be something that had done this to her. And that meant there were more of them.

Like Darkness Himself. He knew too much. Had he been the one to hurt Shiloh?

Reaching to open the cabinet, her hand shook, and she knocked the Band-Aid packet into the sink. It took three tries before she was able to rip the box open and bandage her fingers.

Her head shot up as a loud thump sounded through the ceiling. She raced for the kitchen, sliding a large blade from the knife block. Sidestepping her way up the stairs, she crept along the hallway towards the grunts, gasps, and knocking muffled behind one of the doors. Her palm was sticky with sweat, the metal handle slippery in her grasp. Swallowing against a dry mouth, she opened the door and froze. Her heart stammered in her chest as she found her sister straddling Seth, blood staining the front of his shirt. Shiloh spun her head around, eyes a fiery crimson, and red dripping from her fangs.

Fucking. Fangs.

The knife bounced on the carpet as it slid from Lanie's hand, her body following suit as she checked out on her twisted reality.

———

Oh my God. Oh my God. Oh my GOD.

She'd just sucked on Seth's blood. And *liked* it. She wanted more, the taste of it setting off detonations of pleasure all the way from her throat, through her chest to her core. His flavor, cinnamon and heat, sparked a lust for more than just his blood. She wanted his body stripped and ready for her to feast.

But she was aware that they were in the parking lot, and that her sister was staring, horrified. A scream ripped at her throat, the beast in her protesting the mental shackles she'd enforced.

"*Shiloh*." His lips curled around her name.

She frowned as Seth's hand obstructed her view of the blood dripping from her ear. Realizing how loud she was, she abruptly cut off the sound. The urge to strike at

his vein and drink him dry consumed her with a force she wasn't strong enough to endure.

I have to get away.

Intending only to take a step back, she found herself flying through the air. The incredible surge of energy, intoxicating and damning at the same time. Some force was alive inside her, altering her humanity. Landing on the roof of a car several yards away, she steadied herself before again zeroing in on her food source. *Food source.* She was thinking of her boyfriend as if he were a juicy steak.

Oh, my God. I'm a monster.

Lanie started after her.

"Stay there. Don't come near me," Shiloh warned.

Using all her strength, she bolted away, not caring where she was going, only knowing that she had to get as far away from Seth as she could, or she would end him. And a world without Seth was a world too bleak to contemplate.

She moved with enough pace to make the cars look like they were speeding backwards, her body almost weightless. She was a mere gust of wind stirring up the fallen leaves and skittering abandoned beer bottles across the pavement. The tiny amount of blood she'd consumed had given her a boost of energy as if she'd dosed up on speed. *Imagine if I'd had a proper drink.*

Soon, the suburbs of Los Angeles gave way to nature. The farther she got, the heavier her legs became. The air grew thicker until she sensed an invisible

membrane that stretched like elastic, pulling her back. Back towards him. She fought against it, arms stretched in front, feet grinding into the earth. But she couldn't go any farther. Something had a hold on her.

Lifting her feet off the ground she was flung backwards for several miles, over the tree canopy until she landed, spinning head over tail, and smashed into an old warehouse on the outskirts of town.

She coughed and groaned as her injuries awoke. Shiloh pushed to her feet, her arm hanging at an odd angle from her elbow. She lifted and twisted it back into place with a cry of pain, cradling it against her stomach, almost certain it was broken. Looking around, she had no idea where she was, but the elastic membrane pushed at her back, guiding her in his direction. Refusing it wasn't an option. Even if she'd broken her leg, she would've found her way back to him. Her willpower was spent.

Minutes later she jumped through his bedroom window, finding him sitting on the bed. Shiloh's nostrils flared, the smell of him potent and intoxicating. A tingle in her jaw preceded the elongation of two sharp fangs. She opened her lips to accommodate the sharp points, not giving them a thought because his eyes locked on hers—the greens, yellows, and browns performing a dance just for her. She watched his neck jump in a swallow—the only move he made as he watched warily. Moving to stand between his legs, she adjusted her throbbing arm, wincing at the pain.

He dropped his eyes, concern softening his features, before he scooted back on the bed, giving her room to move over him. When her knees were either side

of Seth's hips, his arms came around to embrace her, chest to chest. Angling his head, he offered up his neck, and she wanted to cry. He didn't know the sacrifice he was making. How could he love her that much that he'd risk repeating her fate?

What kind of animal am I that I'd even contemplate doing this to the boy I love?

His pulse drummed out a beat, the scent of his blood begging her to feast. To embark on an illicit, irrevocable dance and seal them as one.

Her voice trembled. "I might kill you. Or turn you into a monster. But I don't think I can stop myself."

"I don't care. Take it."

She struck selfishly at his neck, dooming him to her will. She only hoped she could stop in time.

Liquid ambrosia poured down her throat, seeping into her cells and arousing a bliss purer than his touch alone had ever done. She drank in great sucking pulls, moaning as he grunted. Her fractured arm began to burn and she broke away, shocked to find that she could move it again. His blood held healing powers. She wanted it all. She shoved his back flat to the bed, slamming her hands either side of his head as she lowered her lips to his bleeding throat.

Click.

The door.

Who dared to interrupt them?

She pulled her fangs from his vein, whipping around to glare at the intruder.

Sister. Lanie.

The bloodlust loosened its hold as she watched her sister drop to the floor, a knife lying beside her. Spinning her head back to see Seth with a blood-stained shirt, eyes fluttering in a bid to stay conscious, the heavy weight of guilt and disgust crushed her to the bed.

What had she done?

Chapter

Six

Bland

"Come on, Lanie, wake up." She patted her sister on the cheek for the millionth time, knowing that she was the last person Lanie wanted to see right now.

Person? More like creature from some bad horror movie. She should just disappear again. But this time it would be permanent. Glancing over at Seth as he slept on the bed, she remembered the membrane forcefully dragging her back to his side and knew it would be

impossible to leave. Maybe there was a cure? Maybe it was reversible? How long would it take to find a way to stop this? How many lives would she endanger? The only way she could make sure her family were safe was if she ended her own life. But there was also the possibility that she'd just turned Seth into a bloodsucker. If he was a danger to her family . . . She shrank away not wanting to think about it.

Crouching in the corner, she hugged her knees, waiting for one of them to open their eyes. Neither of them moved an inch, apart from the subtle rise and fall of their chests. It was the change in Lanie's pattern—a pause before her chest moved faster—that alerted Shiloh to her sister's return to consciousness. Still, she didn't make a move.

"I know you're awake.'

Lanie's hand twitched, probably searching for the knife she'd been holding.

"I put the knife away. You won't be needing that. I'm not going to hurt you. I'm not . . . thirsty . . . anymore." Unfolding her arms, Shiloh pushed to stand.

Lanie rolled away and squashed her back to the door, ready to run.

"Wait. Listen!" Shiloh should've let her run, but if she did it would confirm the worst—that Shiloh had lost everyone and everything she cared about, and she desperately wanted to cling to the speck of hope she had flickering inside.

Her sister flicked a glance at the bed. "Is he dead?"

Shiloh shook her head. "No. He's just sleeping." *Or unconscious.*

"Are you sure about that?"

Crossing my fingers over here. "Yes, Lanie."

Reaching behind, her sister twisted the door handle. "Is he like you now?"

"I don't know."

Lanie curled her shoulders forward, pushing her spine farther into the barrier behind her like she wanted to ghost through it. "I'm sure you'll understand if I don't stick around to find out."

Please don't leave me. "Wait, Lanie. I know you're right to want to run. I don't know if I can trust myself with others, but I do know *you're* safe with me." She winged it, dragging out the logic as she spoke, hoping it made some sort of sense. "Think about it. If this happened to me when I was abducted, then I've been a m—onster . . ." She hated that word. ". . . this whole time. I haven't attacked anyone until now. I never craved anyone's blood until I smelled Seth's. Something about him pulls at me, and I can't escape it. I felt it before, but it's been worse since my return. The only time I've been in control was when he was near. When I touch him, I feel . . . euphoric."

"What if you've turned him into a freakin' vampire and now you need to find some other juice box to suck on?" She bit her lip and pulled the door open. "No offence."

Vampire. A shudder skittered along Shiloh's skin, and her jaw tingled as if reminding her the new additions were still there. It was a definite possibility. Lanie's concern landed a big boot on the tiny flicker of hope she'd been stoking, but it refused to die. There had to be a way.

"I don't know how this works. But I can tell you that I still feel that tug towards him. I can still scent his blood and hear his pulse, and it calls to me. Yours doesn't." That was the truth. She didn't know why. Or if it would continue to be true. But for now, that truth was all she had.

Lanie dropped her hold on the handle, irritation momentarily wiping the look of fear from her features. "What? Am I not juicy enough?"

"Seriously? You are so competitive. Worse than I was. Sorry, but I'm just not that into you."

Crossing her arms, Lanie chewed on her lip. "How do I trust you? You might just be saying that to get me to stay so you can sample the O-positive."

"If I wanted your blood, I wouldn't be able to stop myself. You saw me just now." God, she wished her sister hadn't witnessed that. Pain throbbed in Shiloh's temples as she realized Lanie would never scrub that from her brain. Shiloh had drained Seth until he'd lost consciousness, for Christ's sake. How could she have done that? She didn't deserve to live. "That wasn't me. That was an animal."

She was in the witness stand pleading insanity.

What a cop out. It was you. You're the animal.

Shiloh cleared her throat.

Lanie's eyes roamed Shiloh's features for an eternity before she spoke. "Maybe it's because we're sisters. Our blood is too similar."

"Maybe." *That would be perfect.*

"That's not gonna save me from him, is it?"

Damn. "I don't know if you need to be saved from him, yet. I'm trying to figure out what to do. I should stay here and watch him. Can you cover for me with Mom and Dad?"

"Oh, yeah, sure. I'll just tell them you're on vampire watch." Lanie's eyebrows took a hike upwards.

"Not funny."

"We need to find out who did this to you, Shi. There's at least one more out there. The whole of L.A. is in deep vampire shit if there are more of you." She put her face in her hands and scrubbed up and down. "I cannot believe I'm having this conversation."

"Neither can I." The insanity plea wasn't all that outrageous.

"I want to get the bastard who did this to you, but there's no way a human is going to win in a vampire fight. I saw the way you leapt through the air and zoomed off like a superhero. You'd be cool if you didn't . . ." She pointed a finger at her teeth, ". . . you know."

"Suck on juice boxes?"

"Yeah, that." Threading her fingers in front of her chest, Lanie ran her tongue along her braces. "I'm scared."

"Me, too."

Lanie nodded and awkwardly crossed her arms again, apparently not knowing what to do with them. "I am glad about one thing."

Shiloh's heart leapt, hope swelling with it. "What?"

"I'm glad you don't find me juicy."

Barking out a laugh, Shiloh replied, "You're bland. Like boiled cabbage. I want to vomit just thinking about it." She tried on a smile.

Lanie's eyes popped. "The grin would've worked better without the fangs."

Shiloh's attempt at humor slipped off her face and fell to the floor. "They're not out."

"Yeah, but I know they're there."

Swamped by a sudden sadness, she looked away, her eyes stinging. Her own sister feared her.

The door handle rattled as Lanie took it in her grip again. "I can't be here when he wakes up."

"I know. Go now."

"Be careful."

"I will. Go."

Lanie slipped through the door, her footfalls echoing down the stairs. Shiloh went to the window and watched her sister run across the street and disappear through their front door, doubting she'd ever walk the same path again. The realization turned her heart to lead.

Turning back to Seth, her lead heart fractured down the middle at the possibility of losing him.

She loved her family.

She *lived* for Seth.

Sitting on the edge of the bed, she placed a hand on his arm. His skin burned under her touch. Sweat beaded on his face. The blood-stained shirt was a billboard of accusation she itched to rip off, cleansing him of her sins. His puffs of air tickled her fingers as she trailed them over his chin, the contact still providing the hum of euphoria she craved from him. That had to be a good sign. They still had that connection. Whatever happened, maybe he'd run away with her. If he felt the same pull towards her as she felt towards him then he wouldn't be able to resist. They had to go. It was for the best.

With a deafening roar, he flipped her on her back and had her pinned to the mattress. She didn't have time to react before he'd struck the vein in her neck, his fangs going deep. Locked tightly in his arms, she couldn't move other than slamming her eyelids shut, and flaring her nostrils to drag in air.

Her mind thrust her back in time, unlocking her memory of the attack at the pool. This was exactly how it had felt. The sharp stab in her neck. She'd thought it was a knife or a syringe. But, no. It had been a pair of fangs. Her attacker was so fast she hadn't seen them coming.

This time, she knew what was happening, and who had her in his hold. And this time, she didn't feel like she was drowning in her own blood, and the fire that had accompanied the first strike didn't return.

This time, she was letting her lover take what he needed. And damn if it wasn't exciting to have Seth inside her in this new way.

Adjusting his grip on her arms, he rested on one elbow. His low growl vibrated through her neck as he pressed his pelvis into the cradle of her thighs. His pulls at her neck intensified, infusing her blood with a lust that had her lifting her hips to grind against him. He reached down and lifted her dress, then yanked off her panties. He didn't wait for permission before he unzipped and plunged into her heat. The drags at her neck in time with his thrusts at her core swamped her. He was *everywhere*. There was barely a part of her he didn't touch. One hand traveled up to her face. He slid one finger in her mouth while the rest gripped her jaw. The other hand made its way under her to squeeze handfuls of her thigh in his grasp. His heavy weight pressed her to the bed. Shiloh's breathing became shallow and the panic she'd felt any time they were apart now rose because of his overwhelming command of her body. She wriggled her arms out and pulled his hand off her face. A howl ripped from his chest as he circled her wrist, locking it above her head.

"Seth," she rasped.

His head reared back. His fangs tore from her flesh, and she cried in pain. Glazed eyes, swirling with red and black, glowered at her before sharpening their focus as recognition dawned. Launching his body backwards, he landed in the corner of the ceiling, hands and feet anchoring him to the walls like a spider as his chest surged. Blood dripped from his fangs and chin, adding a fresh coat to the splash of red across his shirt. His shorts

were spread open, exposing his unsatisfied manhood as it pointed at her accusingly.

She sat up, holding a hand to her throbbing neck. He watched her, his face draining of color, making it seem as though the red dripping from his chin was his own. Like he'd sprung a leak. He stiffened, looking around the room before dropping to the floor with a thud.

Shiloh didn't make a sound. She moved her legs inch by inch until her feet could touch the floor, preparing for escape or pursuit. Whatever he decided his next move was, she had to be ready.

Chapter

Seven

Him Again

Lifting a hand, his fingers poked at his fangs, confirming the nightmare she'd trapped him in. Neither of them had had any control over their thirst for each other.

"You turned me." His tone was less accusation, more statement of fact.

"I did. I warned you. I'm so sorry."

"You're sorry? Shit, Shiloh. I just attacked you and you're apologizing." Seth's shorts fell past his knees as he stood. He looked down as he tugged them up, securing the

zipper. "I didn't know what I was doing. Are you okay?" He zeroed in on her neck.

Shiloh lifted her chin, feeling around to find that the marks from his fangs had healed. "Yes . . . are you?" Slamming her eyes shut, she shook her head. "Stupid question. Of course you're not. Sorry. I would say that I didn't know what I was doing to you before, but I did. I just couldn't stop myself. Please don't hate me."

"I don't hate you, Shi. I took the risk because I didn't want to lose you. The way you took off, it freaked me out. I'd do anything to keep you."

"Yeah, like volunteer for a set of fangs. Now both our lives are ruined. I can't go back to my family. I just spent five minutes trying to convince myself and my sister that she was safe with me. But now you're—we're predators. We have to leave." She shot to her feet.

"Whoa, wait a minute." He dragged a hand through his hair, his eyes pleading. "I just fed from you. That means we should be able to keep each other satisfied. Maybe we can hide this from them."

"We can't put them at risk."

"If you disappear again, don't you think they'll have the cops crawling all over the state, if not the country, looking for us? I'll be suspect number-one in your kidnapping. Do you seriously want to do that to your parents and me when all it might take to have a normal life is some self-control and a regular feeding schedule?"

It sounded so simple, but she recalled the raging thirst that had clawed at her throat and seized control of her mind and body. And he'd just experienced the same.

How could she be sure another person wouldn't invoke their bloodlust?

"Maybe. But I don't trust myself after what I just did to you. If it wasn't for Lanie I might not have stopped. I nearly killed you."

He paused, his face hardening for a beat before smoothing out. "I knew the risk."

"You invited the beast. Stupid."

Thunder crossed his features, but he quickly covered it with a grin. "I'm stupidly in love with you." He enveloped her in his arms. "We're going to stay and pretend nothing has changed. I promise everything will be fine. Do you trust me?"

His magic touch filtered through her skin, teasing out her agreement. "I do. And I'm definitely drawn to your blood. I haven't encountered anyone else who does that to me. But if either of us comes close to losing control again, or attacking someone else, we leave straight away. We leave and we never come back. Got it?"

"Good. Let's shower before we get you home."

The picture of her parents slaughtered in their beds still stirred her fears. But as he undressed her, peeling the fabric from her heated skin, he freed her of the weight of her worries. Even if only for a little while, he took it all from her with the drag of flesh upon flesh. Every bite an exchange of nourishment, and a reassurance that their new dynamic would satisfy all of their desires as his blood settled warm in her belly. He flooded her system with a euphoria only he could provide until she was so spent she forgot how to stand.

Thank you, Seth.

I don't want to be here. I don't want to be here.

First day of senior year and herds of students filled the hallway, lockers providing a place to stir gossip or talk crap about each other. Some kids looked like they were about to have a root canal, while others—like Madeline and her bitchettes—worked the space, reestablishing dominance over their subjects.

Everywhere Shiloh and Seth went, heads turned and whispers spilled from loose mouths. Only a few months ago, she would've returned waves and said hello. She would've asked people how their weekend had been and what they had planned for the next one.

That life had burned to ashes and dust, never to be revived. She'd seen the footage of herself stumbling into the gym, looking inches from death. There was no wiping that from people's memories, even if she managed to wipe it from the internet. Thank God she had no memory of that moment. Watching the replay drew out the humiliation and agony she should've—might've—been feeling at the time. But now she knew what *'thirsty'* felt like. She'd never stop reliving her first memory of being in the clutches of bloodlust. The way it had hijacked her mind and body, releasing the monster buried within. As far as Shiloh knew, there were only a few witnesses to that fall from grace. Herself, Seth . . . and Lanie. She'd heard her sister whimpering and thrashing about during the night. If Shiloh could've linked their dreams she'd bet they'd been

replaying the same scene from two different points of view. Predator and prey.

At least no footage from the parking lot had shown up. Either she'd been too fast, or the bystanders had been too slow with their phones. Or maybe they couldn't comprehend seeing a teenage girl flying backwards through the air and landing on top of a car. This wasn't some comic adaptation on the big screen. Things like that just didn't happen in real life.

Shiloh couldn't let it happen again.

Her jaw ached from overindulging in Seth's blood the night before, but she'd had to satisfy her thirst to ensure she wouldn't expose her secret. The beast needed to stay caged. Seth had had his fill so he could keep his fangs holstered, too. This was a huge test. One she'd never wanted to partake in. But Seth had assured her it would all be fine, and she'd succumbed to his charm. The urge to run fought with the trickle of calm feeding through her hand in his grasp as they walked to their lockers.

She wondered how he managed to be so cool. He was a brand-new vampire. They were both new at this. Each person's scent gathered in her nose as she walked by, none of them anywhere near as appealing as the aroma wafting from Seth's skin. She swallowed, remembering the taste of him sliding down her throat.

For the first time, she wanted to pull away. This was way too dangerous.

Keeping her mouth shut, she hugged her books in one arm and freed herself from his grip, pulling the strap of her bag up on the other.

"Babe, do you want me to carry those for you?"

"No, I'm nearly at my locker. I'll be okay from here. I can see my first class. You're going to be late."

He tilted his head, narrowing his eyes before leaning down to give her a kiss. Shiloh waved goodbye with a small smile, watching him disappear into class and breathing a sigh of relief.

As she opened her locker, a flyer fluttered its way to her feet. She snatched it up, reading what it was about. Some movie called *The Lost Boys* was going to be screened in the gymnasium on Friday night. She'd never heard of it. Reading down the page, her blood froze at seeing the word *vampire*. Scrunching it in her fist, she shoved it to the back of her locker and dumped a stack of books in the front, slamming the door.

"Aargh!" She slapped a hand over her mouth to muffle her scream.

Waiting behind the locker door was the dark-haired guy from the mall. "So, you're still with him?"

Fuck. What was he doing here? Was he stalking them? Hadn't he mentioned something about school before he took off? Adrenaline pumped in her veins as her mind raced with her own questions, completely ignoring his query. She'd have dropped her books if she hadn't already locked them away. "What do you want?"

The corner of his mouth tipped up and he leaned his forearm on the locker, crowding her. "I just wanted to welcome you back to school. You know, after your ordeal, and all. Seems like nobody's been real welcoming."

"Um, thanks." *What? Why are you thanking him? Get the hell away.*

"It's Shiloh, right?" His gaze slid from her face farther south and his jaw ticked.

She crossed her arms, her own jaw tightening. Who the hell did he think he was? He'd scared the shit out of her sister and bitten Seth. And now he was trying to, what? Intimidate her? "I have to get to cla—"

"The name's Devlin." Holding out his hand for her to shake, he watched her. Was he for real?

Loose pieces of hair framed his face, but the rest was pulled back in a ponytail. She'd wanted to grab him by that convenient handle and yank him off her sister not so long ago. "You were an asshole in the parking lot. This isn't happening. We are not going to be friends. I've gotta go."

"You have Math first up with Horner."

"Yeah. So? What do you care?" She pulled in some air so she could huff in frustration, but his smell came with it, seasoning it with *yum*. Her fangs tingled. *Shit.*

"I saw your class schedule." He handed her a piece of paper. "You dropped it."

"Uh, thanks." Their fingers touched as he passed her the sheet, the warm current scrambling her mental faculties. It wasn't the same as Seth's caress, but it had an undeniable something—an organic power that spoke to some part of her she didn't know existed. She stepped away and locked it out, lashed by guilt for even

acknowledging the feeling. Seth's was the only touch she needed.

"So, what's he like?"

"Who? Seth?"

"No. Horner. I don't care about your boyfriend."

"I *do* care about him. I can't talk to you." Speeding up her stride, she reached the door to class ahead of him.

He grabbed her arm, stopping her with a jolt. "I wasn't trying to scare your sister. I was having a smoke. She was upset with him."

"Look, I don't want to talk to you. I don't know how else to say it before I start swearing. Back. Off."

Retracting his hold, Devlin put both his palms up in surrender. "I heard you, loud and clear." He retreated a step. "This is me, backing off. But don't ya want to know why she was upset?"

She hesitated for long enough that the corner of his mouth twitched. "If I want to know that, I'll ask her."

"Suit yourself." He swiped a hand over his mouth, covering his expanding smirk, but he couldn't hide his playful eyes or the dancing flecks of green and blue emerging from their dark depths.

A flock of birds took flight in her stomach, delivering a prickle of anticipation to her muscles. Unable to stop herself, she flared her nostrils, taking a long inhale to gorge on his intoxicating smell. It was like smoked chili chocolate with a hint of sin—a mix of spices that would burn all the way down, but make you beg for more. One

hand curled into a fist as she held back a curse. "Ugh. You are infuriating. If you had cornered *me* in the parking lot, I would've punched you."

He moved closer. "I'd like to see you try."

She could run faster than a flash of light. Surely her fist could snap out so fast nobody would see it. It'd be like he fell for no reason. But the shiner might be hard to explain. "It can be arranged."

"Lunch break?"

Her forehead bunched. "Are you serious?"

"As fuck." He stared her dead in the eye before dropping his gaze to her lips.

Shiloh's knees loosened, ready to dump her weight to the floor as her body awoke in all the wrong places. Places reserved for Seth.

It looked like Devlin hadn't shaved around his goatee for a few days, hair shadowing his cheeks. He screamed danger, but she wanted to pull back the cloak and discover his secrets.

"Are you two joining our lesson today, or just decorating the hallway?" The teacher's stern warning pushed them apart.

Devlin's demeanor went from intense to chilled out in a flash. "Hey, Mr. H. How ya doin'?"

"You are three seconds away from a detention, Mr. Vice."

Behind the teacher, the students were all watching their exchange, their whispers rising to a dull roar.

"Nah, it's all cool. I'm done here." Devlin swaggered into class.

The teacher tapped Shiloh on the shoulder before she could get past him. "Shiloh, welcome to senior year. It's good to see you back. I understand you've been through a huge shock. I hope you've had some time to start healing over summer break. If there's anything I can do to make things easier for you, please let me know, or any of your teachers. We're here to help."

"Thanks, Mr. Horner."

He smelled like tuna fish and bagels. She wouldn't have minded it so much before, but now the scent had her on the verge of dumping her breakfast at his feet. She favored a diet of red meat. Preferably rare. And anything with caffeine. She couldn't survive on blood alone.

Sidestepping past him, she made her way to the only free desk, front and center. Dropping her bag on the floor, she sized up where Devlin was, feeling his eyes boring into her from the back of the room. Any hint of complacency was lost in the dark pools of his eyes and the heavy set of his brow. He was pissed. She swore she saw flashes of red in his irises before he turned away.

She spun around, practically lunging into her seat, and shut her eyes. Her gums ached, wanting to release her fangs. She could smell his tantalizing scent from the back of the room, as if he'd turned up the volume on it from ten to fifty. *Crap*. What did that mean?

Covering her face with her hand, she coughed. Her throat was parched, but that was it. Holding both hands out in front of her, she noticed a slight tremble, but no threat

of body-wracking tremors like she'd had with Seth. She was still in control.

That had to count for something.

So why was the thought of diving into his lap to strike at his neck consuming her mind?

Chapter

Eight

Homework

Maybe it was stupid, but she went to the cafeteria, searching for Devlin. When he didn't show up, she walked around the buildings looking in all the places where he might be having a smoke. Nothing. He was a coward. All talk, and apparently, all walk. She embraced the disappointment, hoping it would crush her curiosity. Yep, that was all it was.

Her phone beeped with a text from Seth.

Where are you?

She could feel him near, the pull of their connection drawing her to him. For the first time, she fought against it. There was no way she'd be able to look him in the face without turning flaming red with guilt. She might have to sew a large scarlet letter A to her shirt.

I haven't done anything. I love Seth. I can't leave him. I've already tried that, and look how it turned out.

She huffed out in disgust and headed for the library, tapping out a reply.

Working on a paper. I'll see you after school?

From the door, she could see Lanie's dark head bent over her laptop. Taking a seat at a desk across from her, Shiloh noted the dark circles under her sister's eyes. A notebook covered in scrawl with loose bits of paper poking between the pages sat beside Lanie's computer as she squinted at the screen.

"What are you looking at?"

"Huh?" Lanie lifted her eyes in a daze.

"You're concentrating so hard. What are you looking at?"

"The missing person's database. Did you know more than sixteen and a half thousand kids were reported missing in Los Angeles last year?"

Shiloh's mouth parted. That number was way too many places to the left of the decimal point. And she'd joined the ranks for this year's statistics. What an achievement. "God, Lanie. I don't want to know something like that."

"I wonder how many of them were taken by vampires. I'm trying to find a pattern."

"Like what?"

"If there's a large number of abductions in one particular area we might have ourselves a coven."

Shiloh pulled her chair in closer, witnessing a different side to her sister unfold as she drove the mouse. Lanie had more smarts and determination than she'd given her credit for. Shiloh suddenly felt fiercely protective, wanting to snap the laptop shut and whisk her little sister back home to safety. "What if we find who did this? How are we going to deal with it? The police won't believe us, and they wouldn't stand a chance against our vampire strength and agility."

"Our? You're not one of them, Shi."

"Yes, I am."

"You're still my sister."

Shiloh's heart squeezed and a lump formed in her throat. After all she'd done, Lanie still thought of her as her sister. Not as something to be feared, or as a monster.

They'd grown up trying to outdo each other at everything. Best cook. Fastest runner. Lanie had beat her at almost everything until Shiloh found swimming.

They'd braided each other's hair and raided their mother's secret chocolate stash together. She'd teased Lanie about being a party girl, but had always made sure she got there and home again safe. It eased Shiloh's mind because she knew she'd dropped the ball where Lanie was concerned. She'd prioritized swimming and Seth, and her

relationship with her sister had drifted into distance. Being the designated driver hadn't been enough. She knew it.

You're still my sister.

Lanie still loved her and was willing to forgive.

Shiloh blinked a few times to ward off tears, singling out each drifting dust mote as Lanie's words sunk in. "I love you, too."

"Don't start that. We have to focus."

"You're right. Sorry."

"Most of the cases in California are from Los Angeles. No surprise there, I suppose, due to population alone. I wish I had access to the police files. I'd filter them according to the area where the missing was last seen and maybe cause of death. Surely not all the victims are turned. Maybe some of them die of blood loss. Then there are those like you who've returned, but who are acting weird. Well, weirder than normal."

"What are you whispering about?"

Shiloh twisted in her seat to see Seth flashing a smile that had her wanting to fold into his familiarity. How strange that she hadn't felt him coming. She always knew when he was near ever since they'd met.

"Shiloh's helping me with my history paper."

Liar, liar. Shiloh eyeballed her sister sideways. Why didn't she tell him?

"You have homework on the first day of school? What's the topic?"

Vampires.

"The assassination of Abraham Lincoln." Lanie didn't even twitch, her face as straight as a flagpole. Wow. That was skill.

"Google it. You'll figure it out." Seth's tone had bite.

Shiloh had always known these two didn't like each other, but since her reappearance it was developing into contempt.

He ignored Lanie, resting his palms on the desk beside Shiloh. "Want to come eat with me?"

Her butt rose two inches off the chair before her brain re-engaged. Lanie was hiding this from him for some reason. She'd told her sister about Seth being a vampire. He could be helpful. An extra set of fangs would come in handy in a vampire fight. She decided to go along with it despite the instinct to tell him. "Um, no. Thanks, but I can't. I'm helping Lanes. I'll see you after school?" She broke out in a sweat as every word got stuck on her tongue, protesting its release.

It wasn't like she hadn't said no to him before, especially with her demanding training schedule. But to refuse herself time with him now was like denying herself shelter in the snow. She put her hands in her lap to hide the trembling.

She needed to be with him.

She also needed to find her attacker, and Lanie had the right instincts on this one. Seth needed to be kept out of it. If he found out what they were doing, he'd want to stop her. And he'd want to protect her. Now it was her turn to protect him. She didn't want him hurt.

Lines etched beside his mouth as he eyeballed her. "I'll come and get you after last class."

He took two steps away before whirling back. Holding her by the nape of the neck, he mashed his lips to hers in a mark of possession, and left her panting as he stalked to the door. She gripped the arms of her chair to stop herself from following, but she could've sworn the chair moved a couple of inches on its own, like he had her tied on a string. Like the membrane that pulled her to him was stretching, trying to accommodate this new distance between them. It was in danger of snapping back.

Yes, he was pissed off, but she was doing this to protect him.

They'd be okay.

Spinning around, she found Lanie staring at her. "What?"

Lanie's face screwed up. "He's such a dick. Even more now that he's—"

"Stop, Lanie, okay? You're talking about the boy I love."

"Whatever. It's your business who you choose to be with." She dismissed the argument with a jerk of her shoulders.

Shiloh ground her teeth. "Yeah, it is."

"I think I found a pattern." Lanie cracked a smile, waving her hand for Shiloh to come and see.

All animosity forgotten, she wheeled her chair closer as Lanie pointed to her notebook. "Fifteen people were last seen off Hollywood Boulevard in the few weeks

before your disappearance. Six of them were outside a club called Fluid Prey and the rest, not far from it. It's not much. We're working on limited info here, but it is a pattern. I think we need to check it out."

"How are we going to get into a club without ID?"

"I know a guy."

"What?"

Lanie shut down her laptop and packed up her things as she spoke. "I realize you've been sheltered with your big swimming career, your celebrity status on campus, and your Olympic dream, but some of us grew up in the real world. I know who to go to for drugs. I know who to see for ID. I also know which nerds will do your homework for a price. I. Know. A. Guy."

It was official. Shiloh had failed as a big sister.

———

Lanie bent forward, almost touching her nose to the mirror as she glued her false eyelashes in place. Shiloh had put hers on in two seconds and was now adding a final layer of lipstick. Miss Popular might not be a party girl, but she had admirers and a boyfriend to impress. She knew how to pretty herself up. Lanie didn't give a crap. She had no idea what she was doing, the glue sticking to her fingers more than her eyelids, but she finally got them in place and stepped back to inspect her work.

I look like a hooker.

Sneering at her reflection, she ran her tongue over her teeth, recently freed of their metal binds. The smooth

surface was weird on her tongue, but at least that was one less clue as to her real age.

"You look amazing." Shiloh smiled.

"I look like a tramp. I never could do my makeup for gym comps. How come you don't look like a tramp?"

"Maybe try toning down the blush and go for a pink–rose color on the lips. The fire engine red isn't doing it for you."

Lanie surveyed her sister's reflection. Beautiful. How could she look so like Shiloh and yet still never measure up? "It's working for you."

"Yeah, but I've done a pale cat-eye look on the eyes. You've gone smoky."

"Ugh, God. Sometimes I hate being female."

"Here, let me fix it. Sit down."

Lanie closed her eyes as the soft tissue brushed against her cheek. Feeling the press of her sister's finger under her chin, she fought against the coursing of adrenaline resulting from being so close to a set of fangs. She'd nearly lost this. And although her body instinctively knew that it could be in danger, she'd take a vampire sister over a dead sister any day.

Lifting her lids, her gaze roamed Shiloh's face. Even without makeup her sister's skin was flawless, but since her transformation the pink hues under the surface of her skin had lifted. Her lighter brown eyes stood out, framed with thick lashes and eyeliner. When Seth was around they set off in a rainbow of fireworks. And when she was thirsty, red stained the amber. It wasn't something

you'd notice unless you were studying her closely. If anyone was to catch her drinking they'd see her irises alight with scarlet. But when she went into bloodlust and black consumed the whites of her eyes, that was some freaky shit. She'd only seen it once, in the parking lot.

Shiloh applied a fresh coat of lipstick to Lanie's mouth and straightened, recapping the stick. "Much better."

"Thanks. You ready for this?"

"Maybe you should stay in the car." Shi threw all the makeup back in its case and snapped it shut.

"Not happening."

"But what if you end up like me?"

"I'll have another try at the red lipstick if that happens."

She propped her hands on her hips. "Lanie."

"Shiloh." Mimicking her sister, Lanie exaggerated her voice.

"You are such a pain in the ass, you know that?"

"Learned it from you. Let's go."

Chapter

Nine

Burial

Smoke tumbled out of the door of Fluid Prey as the bouncer ushered them in. Raising her head in awe, Shiloh took in the huge room. From the outside, the building looked as large as a movie studio, big enough to hold the set of *Titanic*. Inside, it had four levels of balconies, each one containing a bar and spaces divided off for separate parties to indulge in whatever pleasures they desired. Elaborate chandeliers hung from the ceiling, and vines twined their way along banisters and up poles. Mirrors lined the walls, giving the reverie a feeling of infinity.

The pounding music made it impossible for the sisters to hear each other as they navigated the crammed bodies gyrating under swirling showers of light. Shiloh's grip clamped onto her sister's arm so hard Lanie had to loosen it. Shiloh mouthed an apology and signaled for them to get off the dance floor and over to some booths at the far end of the expanse.

Jostled between all the sweaty bodies dripping in pheromones, Shiloh's sanity attempted to claw its way out of her skull. *Why do people voluntarily submit to this torture?*

They pushed through, several eyes locked on them while the white flash of teeth glowed brightly under the black lights. Recognizing several famous faces, she understood the exclusivity of the club, wondering how they got in so easily. Suggestive smiles were thrown their way. A shudder wracked Shiloh's body, and she pushed Lanie faster as it became obvious several sets of teeth had extra-long canines.

The place was crawling with bloodsuckers.

How had the existence of vampires remained a secret?

Bursting free of the throng, they sucked in the tainted air, stale with sweat and the output from the fog machines. Shiloh searched the booths for an empty space, her gaze springing back when she scanned past a familiar face. Detective Carter, draped in a silver, sequined, backless dress, and chugging down a weird-looking martini. Perched on the end of the seat, she leaned in to the man beside her and licked up his neck before grinning and bouncing up from her seat, heading to the dance floor.

Shiloh blocked the detective's path. Carter swayed towards her, on the verge of a hug, or a dance. Or maybe just collapsing. Her breath smelled of alcohol, but there was something else lacing it. Surely not drugs. As Carter's arms snaked around Shiloh's neck, over the detective's shoulder Shiloh caught sight of the people sitting at a nearby table popping things—possibly pills, it was hard to see—on their tongues. She doubted they were the complimentary peanuts.

"I know you. Shiiiloh. You smell different. You've been mated. Lucky you. It always makes us smell different." Swaying from side to side, she led Shiloh in a weird slow dance. "Aren't the colors pretty?"

Mated?

Us?

Did she mean vampires?

"What are you talking about?" Lanie stood behind the woman, pulling her arms off Shiloh's shoulders.

Yeah, what was she talking about?

The detective spun out of her hold and threw her hands in the air, squealing in delight. "I love this place!"

Was this the same woman who had interviewed her? Taken Shiloh's bloodied swimsuit as evidence and vowed to find the person who had hurt her? Carter was talking like she knew things. Was it possible that vampires had infiltrated the LAPD?

"What are you talking about, Carter?" Shiloh wanted to shake the woman as a ball of panic swelled in her chest.

"We're never fully satisfied until we find our one. Human blood is bland in comparison, but unfortunately, necessary for Seekers." She glanced at Lanie before smiling widely, revealing her impressive dagger points. "Didn't you figure it out?"

Oh, shit. "Uh, no."

"No, I guess you're still uneducated. Honey, welcome to the club. Nobody gets in here unless they're a vamp, or accompanied by one. You'll soon realize there are thousands of us, living in secret. Don't worry—I made the evidence disappear." She swiped her hands through the air, cleaning an invisible window.

Lanie shoved her face into the woman's personal space, heat rolling off her body in waves. "What evidence?"

"The Chatsworth Quarry dust. It's conveniently missing. Simpson will never find the place," Carter sang the words, clearly pleased with her deviance.

The recollection of her dirt-covered body plastered itself to the back of Shiloh's eyelids and worked to pull out forgotten memories.

"What does the Chatsworth Quarry have to do with anything?"

"Arkose sandstone. It changes color as it weathers. You were covered in it. Don't tell me you've forgotten your birthplace."

Everything slowed before fading away as her mind traveled back in time.

Unable to breathe, she frantically gouged her fingernails into the cold earth, making small tunnels that collapsed back in as fast as she'd made them. Her silent grave pressed heavily on her, creeping into every crevice it could find. Ears. Eyes. Mouth. The sensory deprivation twisted her brain, wringing out the fluid until it was a shriveled nut. But she could still feel. Fighting against her cocoon, she pushed with all her strength until she had enough wriggle room to dig towards what she hoped was the way up.

Her fingers broke the surface, her wrist swinging wildly to widen the gap and gain purchase. Soon it was enough to invite in the fading daylight and air. Stretching her neck towards the light like a sunflower, she evicted the dirt from her mouth and dragged in her first breath.

She waited. Tingles worked their way through her body, amplifying until she quaked with power and burst from her grave with a roar. Collapsing in a heap, she surrendered to exhaustion, thawing her chilled body under the warm sun.

"Fuck."

"You remember." Carter broke out in raucous laughter before dancing off.

"What just happened?" Lanie's gentle touch abraded what was left of Shiloh's patience.

"Get us out of here."

"What—"

"Just do it!" she screamed, her fangs punching out of her gum, piercing her lower lip.

"Shit. Follow me." Lanie led the way, her tiny body shouldering vampires out of their path. If Shiloh had any control she might've been impressed, but her chest heaved like she was buried alive all over again.

Suddenly, bodies started slamming together, collecting in a wall of flesh either side of their path. It was as if some unknown force was holding them to ransom. The loud music was no match for the revelers' terrified screams. The sisters didn't waste the break, bolting towards freedom amid the chaos. The walls collapsed in their wake, bodies falling into Shiloh's heels.

They weren't going fast enough. With her eyes on the door, Shiloh scooped up her sister behind the knees and shoulders, and leaped towards freedom, landing in front of the bouncer. He held up a hand to stop them, and she visualized ripping it off, snapping her head up to spear him with a warning instead.

Her body locked as red washed across her vision of the familiar face. "You."

Lanie jumped out of Shiloh's hold, stumbling back. "No."

Fierce in a long black cloak over black jeans and a tight black shirt, Devlin looked like he'd earned his name the bad way. Eyes ablaze with red, he bent close to Shiloh, dragging his nose a breath away from her lips. Fear had her blood hammering, but she was frozen to the spot.

A deep line carved between his brows as he looked at her. "Contaminated."

Contaminated. What did he mean?

Her heart turned to stone, the affliction spreading like a disease into her ribcage and organs. Another tomb-like confinement under some strange power. Her eyes stupidly pricked with tears.

"Shiloh, let's go!"

I can't. She couldn't move her jaw to say the words.

Blazing red eyes held her in their grip, Devlin's raised hand forming a claw that seemed to squeeze her insides until she felt she'd pop. He dropped his hand, his eyes turning fully black before he was gone.

The stone crumbled from her insides, setting her free. She rocked forward as air rushed into her lungs. People pushed their way past, stampeding for the door.

"Go!" Shiloh grabbed her sister and ran.

Those black eyes.

Devlin is a vampire.

Holy shit.

His irises had burned blood red before the pupils spilled their ink, eclipsing the entire surface of his eye.

She'd never forget the chilling sight.

Lanie had told Shiloh about her black eyes. Was that what she looked like? Had he been hungry? Thirsty for her blood?

Contaminated.

Did he mean her blood was contaminated? He'd almost carved the word in his deep tenor. Set it in stone. Like she had been. Had he done that?

He reeked of evil. What did he want with her? Or had he already had a taste?

The trail he'd made up her neck as he sniffed her scent still tingled. She scrubbed her palm over the skin, desperate to get rid of the sensation.

Not only did the tingle form ice in her veins, it set her alight.

She'd liked it.

Fuck.

Chapter

Ten

Birth

Seth licked her blood from his lips and rolled off her body. "I love your taste."

"I love yours, too." She blinked at his bedroom ceiling, knowing she'd just told him a lie, his cinnamon flavor acrid on her tongue.

Something had happened in that club. A shift in her makeup. A tear in the membrane that tethered her to Seth. The pull was still there, but it had weakened. His taste wasn't the same, and yet it was. She couldn't figure out why.

Spending most of her hours in the seclusion of her bedroom, she'd vary between staring at her trophies—another symbol of what she'd lost, and rubbing at her skin—a futile attempt to rid the remnants of her underground terror from her body.

She'd ripped the bars from her window so she and Seth could regularly feed. Her parents hadn't said anything. They were probably too scared to upset her in case she flipped out again. At school, she searched for Devlin, invariably finding him watching her from afar. Frustration consumed her at being unable to approach him with Seth stuck to her side. He escorted her between classes. She had to peel him off when it was time for him to leave. He wasn't stupid. He knew something was off. Her acting skills were crap.

She just wanted answers.

"Shi?" Seth's finger traced a path down her arm.

She forced herself not to recoil. "Yeah?" Flat. Her voice was flat.

"What are you thinking?"

"I remember."

He sat up, twisting to watch her. "What do you remember?"

"Being buried alive."

He scrubbed a hand through his hair. "Are you serious?"

"Yes."

His shoulders stiffened. "Have you told anyone?"

What? I tell him I was buried alive and he asks if I've told anyone. "Just you."

Bobbing his head, he shifted to sit cross-legged. "Okay. Good. You can't tell anyone. You know that, right?"

Laying a hand on her belly, he trailed it upwards. The sensation she normally felt from his touch was muted.

Swinging her gaze to his, she narrowed her eyes, and he removed his palm.

"We can't expose our secret. If the cops start asking questions again, our cover will be blown."

The LAPD is probably infested with vampires. "Yeah. I guess."

"We'd better get ready for school."

Is that all he's going to say? He's not going to ask how I got out, or if I'm okay? "I'm not going."

He looked at her like she had a toe growing where her nose should be. "You have to."

"No, I don't."

"What are you going to do, then?"

"I need to rest today. I'm tired."

"Do you want me to—"

"No." She bit out her reply before thinking better of it. "No, I'd like to be alone. Thanks."

Standing, she crossed the room to put on her clothes.

"Jesus, Shi. I've done everything I can to help you deal with this and you treat me like shit."

"I just need some breathing space. You've been shadowing my every move." Yanking the T-shirt over her head, she ground her teeth.

"Because I'm looking out for you. Fuck me for caring."

"I have to deal with this in my head, and having you smother me isn't helping. I appreciate you, babe, but this isn't us. You weren't like this before. Let's try and get back to how we were before all this happened."

Blowing a long breath out through his nose, he flopped back on the bed. "Fine. Whatever you want."

"Thank you."

She jumped out of the window and bolted across the street, knowing she was too fast to be seen. After she climbed through her window, she headed down the hallway. Knocking softly on Lanie's door, she hoped her sister was already awake.

"Come in." Dressed in a T-shirt and jeans, Lanie sat at her desk in front of her laptop.

"I have to tell you something."

"Okay."

"I was buried alive. Or maybe I was dead and I … I don't know, came to life or something, but I was in a grave."

Color leeched from Lanie's face as she listened. "Oh, my God. That's horrific."

Shiloh rolled her shoulders as if shaking off the dirt all over again. She needed to purge. Set herself free. "That night at the club, I remembered digging myself out. Detective Carter said something about the quarry being my birthplace. I think I should see it." She didn't want to. She needed to. "The other thing is, if humans are turned into vampires through a bite, what did she mean by birthplace?"

"You bit Seth, and he turned into a leech."

Ugh. She'd rather be called a bloodsucker, or a monster. Leech sounded so … parasitic. "True. Thanks for the insult."

"You're welcome. I printed out a map of the quarry." Lanie got off her chair and grabbed her backpack, taking out a rolled up bit of paper. "It was shut down in 1915 after it supplied tons of rock for the San Pedro Breakwater. It's about twenty-eight miles northwest of LA. I was going to catch the bus."

"I'll drive. But I'm going alone."

"You don't want me to come with you?"

"No. If there are any newborns, they're going to be unstable and might want to suck on your bland blood, but thank you."

Lanie rolled her eyes. "Ha, you need to work on your insults. I want to check something else out, anyway."

"What?"

"I'll let you know if I need to. It could be nothing." She swiveled her chair side to side, running her tongue

along her teeth. "Be safe. Maybe you should take dad's gun."

"Why would I need a gun when I have fangs and superpowers?"

Lanie's eyes crinkled as she smiled wide. "True. Then, be badass."

"Done."

Picking her way around the rocky outcrops, the feeling of déjà vu swamped her. Shiloh had done this before, but had barely been able to walk. Overhead powerlines crossed the landscape, and the railroad cut tunnels into the hills.

She stayed off the walking trails where hikers unknowingly risked their lives from things far worse than a broken neck. Following her instincts, she passed the piles of abandoned boulders from the old quarry and made her way to some hills beyond. Hiking to the top, she had a panoramic view of the valley below under a clear blue sky. From this distance, it didn't look that different from the rest of the quarry. But she could just see disturbances in the earth. Depressions that looked freshly dug out, the soil still dark with moisture, and patches bulging with piles of dirt. Scattered haphazardly between the brush and rocks, it was a mass grave and an earthly womb in one.

Shiloh sat on a rock, buffeted by the return of her memories. She'd crawled on her hands and knees up this hill, trying to figure out where she was. Weak from her ordeal and a lack of sustenance, she'd wished for death,

but had eventually felt the tug towards home and followed it.

To Seth.

Why had she wanted to see him so badly?

I was thirsty.

Awareness that she wasn't alone had her turning to find Devlin standing a few feet behind her.

"I knew you'd come back to see it."

Springing to her feet, she braced her stance, ready to fight. "How did you know I was here?"

"I saw you talking to Sienna. The cop. Her tongue loosens when she's off her face. It usually makes for informative entertainment." He pulled a smoke out of his pocket, lighting up. "Vampire sires always bury their victims where they were born. If you go on to kill, you'll bring 'em here to be reborn. Unless you *want* them to die."

"But vampires are made by being bitten."

"Yes, but if the body isn't drained and buried, it will die without transformation. A vampire has to dig itself out and find its sire for its first feed."

Her phone rang in her pocket.

Lanie.

She pulled it out, answering the call. "Are you okay?"

"Shi, I just found Seth's picture in a missing person's report from two years ago, but that's not his name."

Her eyes shot up to Devlin's penetrating gaze. He stood still, his hair blowing in the breeze as he waited for her to piece it all together.

Eighteen months ago, Seth had moved in across the street.

Why hadn't she ever met his father?

Vampires needed to dig themselves out and feed from their sire.

Seth hadn't been buried. Not by her.

He'd already been turned.

She didn't want to believe it. Briefly clamping her eyes shut she took a mental detour, the thought too heinous to entertain. Still holding the phone, she watched Devlin take another drag of his cigarette. Her number one suspect was staring her in the face. "Where were you reborn?" she demanded.

"I wasn't."

Not reborn? Was he not a vampire?

Her grip on the phone tightened as she swallowed against a cramping throat.

No. Oh, God, no.

"Where was Seth reborn?" She could hear Lanie questioning what was going on as she waited for Devlin's reply.

"Here." He rumbled, gaze locked on hers.

Shiloh's eyes shot towards home as she shouted into the phone, "Lanie, get out of there. Seth is the one who took me."

There was dead silence on the other end of the line. She pulled it away from her ear to check if the call was still connected.

It wasn't.

———

To be continued . . .

Titles

by

J.M. Adele

Coming Home Series

Sensing Series

Sensing You
Convincing You (Coming Soon)
Indulging You (TBA)

Bloodlust Series

Ashes and Dust
Ember and Flame

Read on for a sneak peek at *Ember and Flame*.

EMBER & FLAME

Chapter

One

Polo

Shiloh leapt over the terrain, her ribcage surging for air. Devlin followed closely. Abandoning the car at the quarry, she hit the road, speeding faster than a blink on the smooth surface. She thought of her time with Seth. The declarations of love. The tender caresses. The stolen moments before dawn.

All lies.

He'd been grooming her, and she'd invited him in.

But why? Why had it taken so long for him to bite?

She battled the need to hurl boulders at the earth until a crater formed, a small-scale example of the destruction inside her ribcage.

That had been his voice at the pool before she'd been attacked.

Marco?

Marco?

Marco?

Oh, God. What had he done to Lanie?

They reached the house, finding Lanie's window open. Devlin jumped through first. "She's not here."

Her mood darkened further, lashing out at the nearest target. "Why are you here? I don't need your help."

He ignored her, reaching for the cell phone discarded on the bed.

"Don't touch anything."

The laptop was still open on the desk, its screen lighting up when she tapped the mousepad. Seth's face stared back at her with the details of his description and where and when he'd last been seen. Nearly two years ago, he'd gone missing from downtown LA. And his real name was Jax.

The closet door was ajar, but that wasn't unusual. Creased with the indent where Lanie must've sat during their phone conversation, the bed was otherwise neat. Nothing around the room looked amiss—apart from the gaping window. Lanie didn't like it open.

Seth—no, Jax must've jumped in and snatched her. Lanie wouldn't have even had a chance to scream.

Shiloh sank onto the mattress, her bleak stare aimed out the window to the house across the street. He wouldn't have taken her sister there. Too obvious.

"Do ya still feel the pull towards him?"

Her eyes snapped to Devlin's. Of course! She'd been so worried about her sister and focused on getting to her that she hadn't thought of the connection she had to Seth. They'd always find each other. He wouldn't be able to go far.

Tuning into her senses, she tested the elastic membrane, feeling it stretch. "It's weakened."

"Follow it before it vanishes."

Diving out the window, she tumbled on the grass, springing up to speed off.

"Why is it fading?"

Devlin met her stride for stride. "You've been fighting against his bind since …" His eyebrows dipped as he clamped his mouth shut. "He could be diluting your blood by feeding from another. Or he could break the bond altogether by finding a new mate. The only unbreakable bond is between true mates."

"And we weren't true mates."

"Nope."

Thank God. Sadness tainted her relief. She'd loved him with everything she'd had.

What a fool.

Shiloh and Devlin wove through the streets of L.A. coming to a halt in an alley off South San Pedro Street, Skid Row. Rubbish scattered on the pavement as a cat jumped in fright, hissing at them.

The membrane pulled her another few yards down the street to a six-story brick building. Roller doors covered the windows along the width of the first floor, spray-painted in street art. The pattern was broken in the center by a set of double glass doors, sheltered under a portico. Craning her neck, Shiloh scanned the rows of awning windows, pinpointing where Seth was.

"They're in here. Third floor, back of the building."

"He'll know you're here."

"No point being quiet, then."

"We don't want her hurt. And we don't want to draw attention to ourselves."

Shiloh's shoulders bunched as her gums ached. She wanted to rip out Seth's throat just like he'd done to her. "How do I kill a vampire?"

"With a mortal wound. But you've gotta catch him first."

Going back to the alley for some cover, she bent at the knees and pushed off the ground, aiming for the fire escape. She rattled the window before being pushed aside as Devlin sent his elbow through the glass.

"I thought we weren't drawing attention to ourselves." Shiloh narrowed her eyes.

"Just get inside."

Crunching over the broken glass, she led the way through the rooms strewn with broken office furniture and discarded equipment. Coming to a door, Devlin stepped in front, pushing it open.

Shiloh's lungs seized, trapping her breath. Lanie was perched on Seth's lap, her head lolling to the side and her face swollen with bruises and cuts. One arm was strapped around her waist, and his other aimed a gun in their direction.

A couple of feet to the side, a woman's body lay twitching on the floor, blood seeping from a gaping wound in her neck.

"Polo, you blood-sucking bastard," Shiloh spat, ready to lunge.

"If you come any closer I'll kill her." Opening his jaw wide, Seth tilted his fangs towards her sister's exposed neck. "Even if you bury her, I won't feed her. She'll die."

"What do you want?"

Seth's fiery gaze turned on Devlin. "You know what I want."

"You can't have her."

"Neither can you." A chilling cackle burst from Seth's throat before he turned the gun in a blur, blasting a hole in the head of his twitching victim. The silencer muted the sound, but the vibrations still shattered through Shiloh's body. Pointing the barrel between her eyes, he continued, "Pity your sister's a bitch or I would've chosen her first."

Devlin took a step closer, pulling out a cigarette and lighting it. "You didn't choose her because she's too young. You're stalling. You know ya can't turn her."

What the hell is he doing? Idiot.

Seth switched his aim to Devlin. "Too young to bond, not too young to die."

"Ain't no way you'll kill her. You need her." Devlin peppered smoke rings at Seth's face as he moved in closer.

Lanie moaned, her head moving an inch before flopping back down. Seth reacted by cracking the butt of the gun on the side of her head, and Devlin lunged. In a blinding move, he'd ripped Lanie from Seth's arms and shoved her towards Shiloh. She dove to catch her, eyes half on Devlin holding out a clawed hand. Seth's body was thrown into the wall behind him without Devlin ever making contact. Plastered halfway up the exposed brick like a squished bug, Seth gripped the gun, aiming at Devlin, and pulled the trigger. He stumbled back with a shout, grabbing at his chest where blood spilled down his shirt as Seth dropped to the ground in a heap.

Shiloh's eyes popped, struggling to keep up with what was happening. Adjusting her sister in her arms, she spun and tore out of the building. She needed to get Lanie to safety.

Oh, God. Oh, God. Oh, God.

Sprinting to the nearest hospital, she prayed for Devlin to be okay. Whatever he was, he wasn't human. The way he'd thrown Seth against the wall without even touching him . . . he was powerful. Formidable. Scary as hell. If anyone could end Seth it would be Devlin. She couldn't worry about him. Her priority was Lanie. And looking at her sister's disfigured face she cursed herself for not running faster.

The tug towards Seth still pulled her back and slowed her pace.

The bastard was still alive.

———

"I knew that boy was no good." Her dad whacked the indicator so hard she thought he might rip it off.

You have no idea. Shiloh leaned her head on her palm, watching the suburban scenery whisk by as they drove home. "You never told me."

He grunted and turned into their driveway. "I don't want to leave you here on your own with him still on the loose, but I need to get some things for your mother and sister. Mom won't leave her side, and I'm tempted to handcuff you to me so you can't go anywhere either."

"Dad, I'm tired. I'll be fine. You'll only be an hour or so, anyway. I promise to be good." It wasn't a promise she was planning to keep. As soon as he left, she was going back to find Devlin.

"I'm putting the bars back on."

"Okay. If that makes you feel better." *Won't stop me.*

Or Seth. Jax. Whoever the hell he is.

"I'd rather brick up the window. Even better— we're moving to a remote island."

She almost smiled. "You can't lock me up like a prisoner. I'm not the criminal here."

Setting free a sigh, he turned off the engine and gripped the wheel. Bowing his head, his shoulders started to shake as tears dripped into his lap.

Her heart sank in her chest. "Aw, Dad." Unbuckling her seatbelt, Shiloh leaned over the gear shift, wrapping her arms around his neck.

"I can't go through that again, Shi."

She rested her forehead on his shoulder, cursing the day she'd set eyes on the devil.

Detective Carter had come to the hospital to get her statement, while Lanie lay in an induced coma due to swelling on the brain. Shiloh hadn't told Carter about Devlin, wanting to keep that off the record. But not knowing if he was okay, maybe she should have.

"Let's get inside." Her dad lifted his head, swiping his tears on his shirt.

"Okay."

After she gave her dad another hug and assured him for the fiftieth time that she'd be okay, he finally left. She dashed up the stairs, swinging her bedroom door wide.

Devlin. Sprawled across her bed, he was playing with one of her trophies. He looked one hundred percent intact, although she'd witnessed the bullet hitting him in the shoulder. If he'd been fed, he was probably already healed. Who knew what he was hiding under his clothes and inside his skull. She didn't want to know.

Liar.

The potent smell of his blood permeated the air and awoke her hunger, but she fought against it. She'd be damned if she let the beast inside her rule over her will. That only led to misery and vulnerability at the hands of predators far more dangerous than her. Devlin had been hurt, blood staining his shirt. That was the only reason the lure was stronger, more intoxicating.

Delicious.

She cleared her throat and jammed her hands on her hips. "Are you okay?"

"Yeah." His eyes flickered with red, a clear sign he was lying, but if that's how he wanted to play it she was willing to move on. She had a million questions that needed answers.

"Good. Then, start talking."

Acknowledgements

I originally wrote this for the Essentially Australian Romance Anthology, dedicated to Aussie authors showcasing what we're all about. Obviously, I had to be a part of it. Sadly, the anthology is no longer available. Thank you to Melissa Bell and J. Thiele for organizing that fantastic collaboration. And thank you to the participating authors. It was a blast.

This little novella has turned into something more than I ever thought it could be. I'm so glad I decided to stretch myself and get a little freaky - er. To my reader group, my Gems, thank you for coming along on the journey with me. Your input has been invaluable. I'd be lost without you. Sorry for being a pest! Special thanks to those of you who volunteered to be beta readers, or ARC readers. Mwah xx!

Lauren Clark . . . wonderful Lauren. What a brilliant editor you are. Thanks for pushing me to be better and go deeper. It's just what I needed. That, and a swift kick up the butt. Challenge accepted for the next one!

Fiona, from Fiona Dreaming and Proof Reading, thank you for slotting this in with very little notice, and for doing a fantastic job.

Huge thanks to the book bloggers who share their love of reading with the world and help authors spread the word about our labors of love. You are awesome. I know how much work you put in. I see you. Thank you!

My wonderful family and friends have been so supportive of all my efforts and my fanciful dream chasing. I am truly blessed to have you all in my life.

My gorgeous guys . . . you are everything. Never, ever, EVER read this. EEEEVVVVVEEEERRRRR. Love you to bits times three.

To all of you reading this right now, thank you for giving this story a chance. I hope you enjoyed it. I wrote it for you. :) Please consider leaving a review, let me know what you think.

About

the

Author

Former nurse, reluctant romantic, and serious reading addict, J.M. Adele, is the author of paranormal and contemporary romance, and romantic suspense. After years of indulging in her addiction to reading, her own characters started to tell their stories. They were relentless, forcing her to put pen to paper and release them into the world.

On most days you can find her juggling motherhood with authorhood while carrying a book in one hand. When everyone else drifts off to dreamland, she escapes into the worlds conjured by the characters in her head.

Follow J.M.

Links to my newsletter and my Facebook reader group
can be found on my website.

   www.jmadele.com

   www.facebook.com/authorjmadele

   @JMAdeleBooks

   @j.m.adele

www.ingramcontent.com/pod-product-compliance
Lightning Source LLC
Chambersburg PA
CBHW020620120726
47905CB00003B/878